He reached down to the bottom of her wet shirt and pulled it slowly above her waist.

His hand skimmed along her flesh, causing her to shiver. Upward, ever so slowly. He stopped just before the shirt crossed over her breasts. "This is where I stop, Joanna, or go on, depending on what you want. It's tonight for us. Maybe tomorrow or the day after, but..."

She knew the rest, and it didn't matter. She wanted tonight more than anything she could remember wanting in her life. And if that was all there was, so be it. Raising her index finger to Chay's lips, Joanna sucked in a quivering breath. "It is what it is, Chay. I understand that. So this is where you stop talking and start paying." She took hold of his hand and guided it under her wet shirt to her breast. "And if it *is* only tonight, make tonight count."

THE
MEDICINE MAN

BY
DIANNE DRAKE

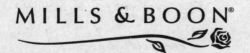

MILLS & BOON®

First published in Great Britain 2005
Harlequin Mills & Boon Limited,
Eton House, 18-24 Paradise Road, Richmond, Surrey TW9 1SR

© Dianne Despain 2005

ISBN 0 263 84314 9

Set in Times Roman 10½ on 11½ pt.
03-0605-55218

Printed and bound in Spain
by Litografía Rosés, S.A., Barcelona

CHAPTER ONE

SOME things never changed. The old road leading from no-where, going to nowhere was still dusty and desolate. The weather-beaten sign reading WELCOME TO HAWK RESER-VATION, POPULATION 3000 hadn't seen a coat of paint on its gray, rotting boards since the first time he'd left here eighteen years ago. The rusty old hull of a 1972 Ford pickup truck that was sitting off to the side of the road had been there since the last time he'd left…left here for good eight years ago.

No, some things never changed, and already Chayton Ducheneaux was missing his morning cup of proper coffee and a quick read-through of the *Chicago Sun-Times*. Certainly, Hawk would have coffee of some sort, something basic and strong, barely drinkable. But the reservation's ver-sion of the *Sun-Times* was a once-a-week, four-page edition of local news. That is, if Will Two Crows was up to putting it out. Most weeks for the past thirty years Will had met his editorial deadline, and most likely he still would for the next twenty or thirty years to come, because, like everything on Hawk, Will Two Crows didn't change much either.

As did every other grown man on Hawk, Will worked the ranch. Hawk Cattle Ranch was owned co-operatively by the smattering of tribes throughout the reservation—the Assiniboine who were Canadian transplants, a small group of Cheyenne on the southern border of Hawk, and the Lakota Sioux—his tribe. By population, his tribe was the majority in the seven small towns that made up the entirety of the reservation. Seven small towns, the largest boasting a population of only seven hundred, and all those towns spread out over nearly two thousand square miles, with only dirt trails and patchy roads connecting them.

Seven small towns, three thousand people. Chayton almost cringed, thinking about it. Hell, his medical practice had more than three thousand patients in it. Talk about reducing the statistics to the barest elements. Chay was beginning to feel agoraphobic. Too much open space here to suit him.

Travel one hundred and fifty miles from civilization, turn right and this was what he got—the same thing he'd left so long ago. Chay looked down the long expanse of God-forsaken road ahead of him, trying to decide what to do. Should he, shouldn't he? This was the turning-back point, if he wanted one. His last chance. He could go back to Billings, Montana, catch the next plane home to Chicago, and be back in the OR by tomorrow morning. Or he could go forward, down that long dusty road to Rising Sun to face the family that had shunned him these past years.

The easy choice should have been to turn around, but his grandmother, Macawi, had sounded so serious when she'd called last week that he hadn't had the heart to tell her he didn't want to come. ''Your father is ill, Chayton.'' Macawi would not have gone against the family to call him home if she hadn't been so desperate. ''He won't listen to anyone, he won't get help. He refuses to see a doctor.''

Macawi. Chayton smiled, thinking about his grandmother. In the Sioux language her name meant *generous*, and that she was. Generous, loving, small and feisty. She'd taken the American name Marie to go along with the family name Ducheneaux, and in the outside world she was Marie. But here at home she insisted on the use of her Sioux name, even when so many others were giving up that tradition. Except him. Chayton, *falcon*, was a good name. He liked it, and even though he had spent so many years away from Hawk, his name was a mantle he still carried proudly, much like Macawi did. The single token in his otherwise typical Anglo life—except for his looks, that was. But they weren't so much a token as a reminder.

It would be nice to see Macawi again, he thought as he put his rented BMW in gear. For a day or two at the most. He'd make his obligatory visit to the ones who would re ceive him, get rebuked by his father, then go home where he belonged. A simple trip, really. Short, but not too sweet.

The road leading into Rising Sun was pretty much like the road leading back out of it. A big, open, desolate prairie, lots of sky, a few scrub bushes, grass. It took some getting used to, having so much nothing all around. He remembered his first trip home, after he'd been sent to the community college up in Fort Peck to study agriculture. Fort Peck, a much larger reservation with the same kind of Indian make-up as Hawk, had seemed like the biggest place in the world to him at the time. There were brand-new buildings, a the-ater for movies, modern schools—he'd eaten his first pizza there. Then he'd come home to Hawk on holiday, and to his own little town of Rising Sun, and had thought he was going to die of boredom. There was nothing, absolutely nothing here, and when he hadn't known better it had been good enough. But once he'd tasted a bit of the outside world, the craving had set in.

And so here he was back in Rising Sun—the same now as it had been then. The main street, called Main, was a wide, dusty expanse, all of three blocks long. No stoplights, no stop signs at the intersections because there wasn't enough traffic to warrant the expense or the upkeep. Chay saw his mother's diner as he passed through the first block. Wenona's, open daily for breakfast and lunch. He'd prac-tically grown up in Wenona's, drinking cherry cola and washing dishes in the back room. As a boy, his friends had gathered there after school and on weekends for a lack of anyplace else to go, and visitors to Rising Sun always stopped there. That had been the best, listening to the outsiders, because sometimes he'd snatched glimpses of the world from them, glimpses he'd most often got from school books. And hearing about places like Chicago, New York, London or Paris was so much more exciting for a kid than reading the flat words on a flat page. Who knew? Maybe it was all those outsiders who'd given him the burning desire to go out and see for himself. And he had seen for himself all the places he'd dreamed about—Chicago, New York, London, Paris and so much more.

He smiled, glancing back in the rear-view mirror at his mother's diner. Of all the places in town, Wenona's was the one that held the most, and the best memories for him.

Wenona...she would be cordial. She would greet him as a mother should when his father wasn't around. And she would treat him as his father dictated when he was. That had been the order of things for eighteen years now, and even though Macawi had had high hopes that the situation might have changed, it hadn't. Chay knew that.

The second block, which was only three buildings long, consisted of a dry goods store, the same one that had always been there, a library and a...Well, what do you know? Chay thought. A pizza restaurant with video rentals. Maybe things were looking up for Rising Sun after all.

First building in the third and last block was the medical office. His first destination. Pulling to a stop in front of it, right alongside a run-down, rusty Jeep, he looked up the half-dozen steps at the person standing at the top, staring down at him. In the midday glare all he could make out was red hair. It was poked up under a baseball cap with only the shoulder-length red ponytail hanging out. She was definitely not a native.

"Dr Ducheneaux?" she called. "Dr Chayton Ducheneaux?"

He pulled off his sunglasses and tossed them into the seat next to him. "And you are?"

"Dr Joanna Killian." She ambled down the steps and stuck her hand through the window to shake his.

"Glad to meet you, Dr Killian."

"Look, I've got to go make a house call. Out in Steele. Everything you need is in the office, and the first patients won't arrive until you call Ruth Young Bird Belcourt and let her know that you're ready to start to work. She's the first patient you'll see—allergies. Normally she does fine with a mild antihistamine. Anyway, she'll spread the word that the clinic's open for business this afternoon, and everybody scheduled will show up. Her phone number's on my desk, by the way."

Chay heard her rambling on and on, but the words weren't sinking in. Did this lady actually think he was there to work in her clinic? "What the hell are you talking about, Dr Killian?"

"Your clinic hours. We've been scheduling them for you ever since we knew you were coming."

"Whoa, lady. I'm not here to be a doctor. I've come to see my grandmother and a few other family members. She told me I'd be staying here at the clinic since it wasn't in use much but I'm not—let me repeat, *not*—seeing patients and I don't know where the hell you would have gotten a crazy idea like that."

Joanna swiped impatiently at a few hairs straying out of the confines of her cap, then bent even further into the BMW. "Your grandmother told me you'd exchange medical favors for staying in the room above the clinic. I assumed that to mean you're here to work. And right now, Dr Ducheneaux, I don't have time to stand here and argue with you. Steele's a twenty-minute drive and I have a broken leg to take care of. I've got ten patients expecting to see you some time today, nothing serious that I'm aware of, and I'd appreciate it if you would oblige me this one favor. Then we'll call it even. OK?''

"Not OK, Dr Killian."

She backed out of the car and stood up. "Fine, Dr Ducheneaux. Suit yourself. But if anybody comes by, will you at least tell them I'll be back this evening, after I treat a broken leg in Steele, hop over to Whitestone and see a new mother about her baby's croup then come through Flatrock to spend an hour or two giving flu shots on my way back here? Tell them I won't get back until late—that if it's urgent I'll see them tonight, if it's not urgent they'll have to come see me first thing in the morning. Starting at six. Oh, and Dr Ducheneaux, make up your own damned bed. I didn't have time."

What a temper, Chay thought as he watched her hop in her Jeep, kick up a dust storm as she threw it in reverse, then barrel out of town. Cute as hell. Small—probably not much over five feet tall—wild, red hair, gorgeous green eyes. Had he seen a smattering of freckles across her nose? Cute as hell, but not the kind of hell he wanted to put himself through. Dr Joanna Killian was a lady with a mission, and he was a man who'd given up crusading a long time ago.

Joanna was halfway to Steele before her temper finally began to let up. She didn't have time to be angry, not with the whole of Hawk Reservation depending on her. Circuit doctor—the ad in the medical journal had sounded appealing when she'd answered it. *Would you like to set your own hours? Do you love to travel? Then come practice medicine in the Big Open.* That was the name for this part of Montana because that's what it was. Big and open. That detail of the advertisement hadn't been deceptive. Setting her own hours was, though, because basically, they added up to every day, all day. Lots of travel could have been a plus point to the job, except they hadn't mentioned that there weren't always roads on which to travel, and most of her destinations were not sufficiently large to earn even the tiniest of dots on the map.

But it was her medical circuit to tend now. Back and forth from place to place, and once in a while she slipped in a day off purely for sleeping. So maybe she should have taken a little better heed when the offer had come within days of her application and they had seemed so anxious to get her. Too anxious. No one had been giving any kind of medical care to the people who lived in the isolated eastern regions of Montana for well over a year now. The last couple of doctors there had lasted only a few weeks, then run straight back to civilization, leaving most of the people with no medical care at all, and the ones who had needed it a long, long drive to seek it out.

So she'd seen the ad for a circuit doctor and had jumped at it because she'd wanted to get away from her old life, her former marriage, any way she could. And here she was, spending more time driving than doctoring.

But the doctoring, when she got to it, was so good, so rewarding, it made all the driving worthwhile.

When Macawi Ducheneaux had stopped by to see Joanna a few days ago and had told her that her grandson, the doctor, would be here soon to help, that had been Joanna's dream come true. Another doctor to share the load. At least that's what she'd assumed. Why, she'd even given him her bed, and been happy to do so. Anything to make him comfy. Not that a lumpy mattress was much of an inducement to keep anyone there for any length of time. And Macawi had said it was only for a short visit, but Joanna would take any help she could get. And her lump-filled mattress was the best she had to offer.

Another doctor to share the load... Yeah, right. More like *he* was a load. A load of pure worthlessness and pretense.

Showing up in a BMW convertible out here. She almost laughed aloud over that one. This country was four-wheel-drives and pickup trucks all the way. His little Beemer would get swallowed up by a dust cloud if he wasn't careful. Yep, Chayton Ducheneaux was definitely all worthlessness and pretense.

Good-looking, though, she decided, thinking about her first glimpse of him. Even though he'd been stuffed into that little car, she could tell he was taller than his family, probably a couple inches over six feet tall. Naturally, he had dark skin, dark eyes, plus a nice muscular build from what she'd been able to tell in her brief encounter. His hair was black, of course, styled in a crisp, short cut. Most of the older men she'd encountered on Hawk here stuck to the old ways—long hair pulled back into a ponytail or a braid. The younger men went both ways, long hair or short. None quite so *GQ* as Chayton, however. Having been married to some-one with the same proclivities, she recognized a fifty-dollar haircut when she saw one. And she'd seen one on him. That, plus manicured fingernails.

Come to think of it, what would have ever given her the silly idea that he would come all the way out to nowhere to work? He was like her ex-husband, Paul. Caught up in the lifestyle. She hated people like that. Especially doctors!

Pulling to a stop in front of Fred Red Elk's house, Joanna waved at Fred's eight-year-old son, Michael. He'd fallen off a horse, suffered a minor break to his leg and, after eight weeks, was hobbling along nicely now. One more check and Michael would be turned loose to play with the other boys— on a limited basis for starters.

"Can I please go do something now?" Michael begged. "It works, it doesn't hurt."

She would have liked another X-ray to be safe, but the Red Elks had neither the money to have it done nor the time to take Michael somewhere to get one. So it was all instinct on Joanna's part. Minor break, eight weeks ago, no pain, no swelling. And the kid was driving his mother crazy. Time to untether him. "If it hurts at all, you have your mother call me," she warned him. "And take it easy for another couple of weeks. No dirt bikes, no horses."

"Can I play football?"

"Can you play something a little less rough instead? Maybe baseball?"

"I hate baseball," he complained.

Cute kid. Dark skin, dark eyes like everybody else. And so full of mischief it fairly sparkled all over him. "Football in a few weeks, Michael. OK? If you go easy for a while."

"But they'll call me a baby, DocJo," Michael whined.

Dr Joanna had become Doc Jo, had become DocJo, one word. She liked that. The lack of formality showed a certain amount of friendly respect she'd been told she wouldn't receive, being an outsider. At least it was a first step in the long process of proving herself. "You tell them I'll be around in a couple of weeks to give everybody shots, with great big needles, and then we'll see who the real babies are." She handed him a sucker, her tradition with all the kids she saw, then shooed him off the porch while she motioned for his mother to come outside.

Betty Red Elk had six other children, and looked frazzled, as any mother of six would look. Like most of the women on the reservation, she was a stay-at-home mom. Scooted the kids off to school in the morning, cleaned, cooked, then greeted the kids when they came home from school in the afternoon. Since it was August and school was still on break for the summer, she merely shooed them out the door and prayed they'd stay outside long enough to give her sufficient time to get her chores done. Then later, when the kids came home for the day and her husband returned from his job at the cattle ranch, she served supper, then she cleaned some more before her day was over. Day in, day out. And the pleasant smile she always wore on her face revealed such a deep contentment with her life Joanna was almost envious. It was certainly a contentment Joanna had yet to find in her own, though it was one she was definitely looking for.

"Restrict Michael to light play for now," she instructed Betty. "I'll be back next week to make sure he's well enough to play football. And he could use multivitamins. In fact, all of your kids could use them. Just some of those chewables that look like cartoon characters. One every day."

"Where can I get them?"

The big question. Certainly no place on Hawk. Rising Sun was the largest town and it didn't have a good medicine supply in its meager pharmacy. Maybe up at Fort Peck, or over in Billings? That was the problem out here. Nothing was convenient, not even a vitamin tablet. And if it wasn't convenient, it was probably forgotten. "Look, I'll find them and bring them when I come next week." Then the Red Elk children would take them until the supply ran out, and Betty wouldn't ask for them again because she was a proud woman who didn't like to inconvenience others.

So many little stopgap measures going nowhere. And the only doctor was always on the run and too busy to finish off all the details, the ones that weren't critical.

Climbing back into her Jeep, ready to drive another twenty miles to see her next patient, Joanna thought about Chayton Ducheneaux settling himself into *her* bed. One thing was for sure—she wouldn't have given it up to him if she had known he hadn't come there to work.

Chayton glanced around the room. Small, basic. An efficiency apartment, only one that lacked real efficiency. Bare necessities, basically. Tiny kitchenette, tiny bathroom, a simple sheet strung across the room separating what appeared to be the bedroom, since it contained a bed, from the living room since it contained a chair. That was it, and Dr Killian was right. The bed had no sheets. They were folded in a pile at the foot, sitting next to a pair of... What the hell were those? Bunny bedroom slippers?

Picking up the bunnies, he regarded them for a moment, then dropped them to the floor. Either an odd welcome gift, or Dr Killian had left something behind. Meaning this was probably where she stayed when she was in the area.

He glanced around, looking for other personal effects, but the room was sterile. Shutting his eyes, Chay tried to focus on the sweet scent of Joanna, the one he'd caught just a hint of while she had been bent over and leaning halfway into his rental car. But nothing. Not even a lingering trace of her.

Not that he wanted a trace of her, because he had an idea that Joanna Killian, with all her expectations of him, was going to be just as big a bother as everybody else here, who would either snub him for not coming home to practice medicine or chastise him. "Why the hell did I even bother?" he grumbled, heading down the stairs on his way out to see his mother. Now was the perfect time since his dad would still be at work and Wenona would more likely be glad to see him when Leonard was away.

"Where's DocJo?" a tiny voice asked.

Chay scanned the cramped waiting area at the bottom of the stairs and saw the waif kneeling in a corner of the room, clutching a generations-old Barbie doll. "Who are you?" he asked, already knowing he'd made a big mistake. Asking meant she'd answer, meant he'd be expected to do something. Treat her, take her home, figure out what she was doing there. Far too complicated for what he had in mind.

"Kimimela Rousseau."

Chay smiled. A name like his, Indian mixed with French. The remnants of the French explorers who'd passed through over three hundred years ago comingling with the natives who had always been there. "Kimimela…"

"It means butterfly."

"Well, tell me, Little Butterfly, what you need."

"I need DocJo. She can fix my finger." Kimimela held up her index finger for him to see. On the end was a tiny little cut, one with a speck of dried blood still clinging to it. "And I can pay," she said proudly. Here at Hawk, not everyone could. "DocJo always fixes me."

DocJo was probably Dr Joanna, he guessed. "Want me to take a look?" he asked, knowing he shouldn't. But it was only a cut. Two minutes to take care of it, then he'd lock the door so no other little butterflies could float in. "I'm a doctor just like DocJo," he added, maintaining his place on the opposite side of the room.

Kimimela frowned stubbornly at him. It was a look that plainly told Chay she didn't believe a word he said. Smart kid, he thought. "Where's your mother, Little Butterfly?"

"At work. She works for Mrs Wenona."

"Mrs Wenona is *my* mother," he said. "In fact, I was just going to see her at the diner. Maybe I could fix your finger then you could show me the way."

"Don't you know where it is?" Kimimela was beginning to show a little interest now. Her dark eyes weren't shining quite so warily at him.

"It's been a long time since I've been…" He caught himself before he said *home*. This wasn't home any more. Home was a nice, luxurious condo overlooking the lake-shore in Chicago. Home had a Jacuzzi, an exercise room, a game room. He looked around. One room in his home was bigger than the entire clinic. "It's been a long time since I've been here. I really need someone to show me around." Back home, a child as young as Kimimela—what was she, maybe six or seven?—wouldn't have been safe walking the street alone or talking to strangers. Of course, in Rising Sun, and even throughout the whole of the Hawk Reservation, no one ever thought otherwise. This wasn't like the outside world. It wasn't even like the rest of Montana. "Come on, let's get it cleaned up so you can show me how to get to Mrs Wenona's."

It was a quick fix—a little washing, a little antibiotic cream, and a bandage. He found a blue one in Joanna's medical supplies, with cartoon characters on it. As he applied it to Kimimela's finger, he vowed that this would be the first and last medical practicing he'd be doing in Rising Sun.

"Don't I get a sucker, Doc Wenona?" she asked, surveying her finger.

He chuckled. "Chayton. My name's Chayton. And if you know where DocJo keeps the suckers I'll be happy to give you one. In fact, if you can find them, I'll give you two if you promise not to tell on me."

Of course, Kimimela knew exactly where they were. She took the two she wanted and looked up at him as if he might up the ante to a third. What the hell. "Grab a handful, Kimimela. As many as you can get in one try."

"DocJo says only one."

"But DocJo isn't here and I say it's OK. OK?" A cheap thrill for a little girl who looked as if she was desperately in need of one. Her little hand scooped up about six suckers in total, and the look of pure excitement over catching such a glorious treasure was well worth the consequences if DocJo actually took such things seriously. Which she probably did.

"Now, do you have something for me?" he asked.

Kimimela nodded, pulling a quarter out of her pocket. She held it up to him, smiling. "See, I told you I could pay."

A quarter. Certainly, he could have turned it down. Most people probably would have. But Kimimela had come there today with such pride he could do no other than send her away with her pride intact. "That's exactly what I was going to charge you," he said. "How'd you know that?"

Kimimela giggled. "I just guessed."

"Well, you guessed good, Little Butterfly. Now, can I hire you to show me how to get to my mother's diner?"

She nodded shyly.

"And how much am I going to have to pay you?"

"A quarter."

"Well, you're in luck. I just earned a quarter myself, so I have enough money." He handed her the quarter, which she tucked back into her pocket. "Ready?"

In answer, she took hold of his hand and pulled him toward the door. *Big mistake, letting the cute kid get to you like this. Keep away from it, Chay. This isn't your life any more.*

"Come on, DocChay," Kimimela urged. "Hurry."

Hurry, indeed. But toward what?

The lump in his gut told him he wasn't going to like the answer.

CHAPTER TWO

HIS mother hadn't changed much, Chay thought. No wrinkles that he could see from where he was standing on the sidewalk outside her diner. No gray hair. Still plump with a flawless round face. Wenona Ducheneaux looked exactly like she'd looked the last time he'd seen her, and he felt the pull at his heart over missing her. He had. Badly.

Eight years was a long time to be away and he was nervous about stepping through the door because he couldn't start over, and he couldn't pretend this was where he'd left off years ago. He was the outsider now, the one who could bring tales of Chicago, New York, London and Paris to Kimimela.

Kimimela wandered on inside, but once the diner door was open Chay couldn't budge from the spot where he was standing. Not yet. So he stayed at the window and watched his mother through it as he grappled to find the words a prodigal son would say after so long. It wasn't like he hadn't talked to her in all this time. He'd called her dutifully every month or so, sent her gifts and cards on all the right occasions, had even offered to fly her to Chicago any time she wanted to come visit him. But she wouldn't, not without her husband. And Leonard Ducheneaux had shed himself of a son years ago.

"DocChay, you coming?" Kimimela asked from the doorway. "I already ordered us cola. And I don't have to pay. Mrs Wenona never makes me pay. Do you like cola?"

"I love cola," he said, finally taking her hand and heading through the door. Inside it was cool. Air-conditioning. Something new since the last time he'd been here. Back then the only cooling had come from overhead fans. He remembered how they'd clicked when they'd rotated. It was a loud, steady noise people got used to and ignored. They were still there, but not running, he noticed, glancing up at the ceiling. Somehow he almost missed the old familiar racket they'd made. "So, where are we going to sit?"

"At the counter. On the end. That's my special place. And you sit next to me."

The diner was bustling. It was lunch and the specialty, he noticed on the chalkboard, was bean soup and corn bread. Of course it was. Today was Tuesday. Tuesday was always bean soup and corn bread. He hadn't had bean soup and corn bread since the last time he'd been here, and suddenly he had a taste for it. Funny how he hadn't thought about it all these years, and now he could hardly wait to sit down at the counter and order a bowl. "Did you order cherry syrup in your cola?" he asked Kimimela as they made their way over to the counter.

"You can do that?"

"You bet you can do that. And it'll be the best darn cola you've ever had." His mother hadn't noticed him yet. She was busy at the other end of the counter, taking an order. Reaching into his pocket, he pulled out two dimes. "When I was your age I could always get a free cola, but I had to pay a dime to get the cherry syrup. That was the rule."

"Chayton!" Wenona's squeal drowned out everything else in the diner and suddenly the place went deathly quiet. All eyes turned toward him and no one so much as moved. "I can't believe you're home. Is that really you?"

"It's me, Weeko." *Beautiful.* By the time he'd stood, Wenona had run around the counter and was flying into his arms.

"It's been so long," she cried. "And I didn't know you were coming. Why didn't you let me know?"

"I didn't decide until yesterday." Although he'd been

thinking about it for a week now. "And it was too late to call. You were home by the time I made up my mind." He bent down to give her an affectionate kiss on each cheek, then said, "I was having this huge craving for bean soup and corn bread, so I thought, why not? You'd be serving it today, and nobody makes it better than you."

Wenona backed away, brushing a few tears from her cheeks. "I know you're lying to me, but I don't care. I'm just so glad to have you home again, it doesn't matter why you came." She glanced around the diner anxiously. "But this is a real bad time. Everybody likes to come in since I got the air-conditioner, and we're really busy. Then I have to get home to your father. He comes home earlier from the ranch these days, and likes to have his supper on the table when he gets there. So maybe we could visit in the morning. Over breakfast? That is, if you've come to see me."

"Of course I've come to see you. You and Macawi and a few old friends, if any of them are still around." Some had gone to the cattle ranch, but many had gone out into the world, seeking other opportunities. That was the way now. Many left and, like him, didn't return.

"And your father? Will you see him, too?"

The old wound. His mother lived ever hopeful that the wound would heal. He didn't have that same hope, though. And as for seeing his father, Chay simply didn't know. "I don't think Dad will care one way or another that I'm here."

"He might, Chayton. He's gotten tired. Time has changed him in so many ways."

Is that what Macawi meant? he wondered. "We'll see, Mom. But I'm not making any promises. So, since I can't sit and visit with my favorite girl in the world, could you at least rustle me up an order of your Tuesday special and get me and my other girlfriend here a cherry cola? It's still a dime for the cherry syrup, isn't it?"

"You've met Kimi?"

He nodded. "She came to the clinic, needed a little medical attention."

"The clinic? Joanna's medical clinic?"

"It's a long story." Eighteen years' worth of 'long' that suddenly seemed even longer than that. "I would have stayed at Macawi's but she's renting her spare bedrooms to a few paying tenants—wives of workers at the ranch—which leaves me staying in the room above the clinic. I was getting settled when Kimimela came in and paid me for my medical services."

"Then *he* paid *me* for *my* services," Kimi chimed in. "And DocChay's paying for my cherry syrup, too."

"Little Butterfly and I are on our first date," he said, winking at Wenona. "The gentleman always pays for the lady's cherry syrup. I leaned *that* from the wisest lady I know." Chayton leaned down and kissed his mother lightly on the forehead. "It's good to be here, Mom."

He said the words, and for the most part he meant them.

Flu shots. Late August was a little early in the season for them yet, but Joanna took advantage when she had the vaccine available to her. And right now she had enough to get through most of those in Flatrock who wanted the shots. Not that everybody did because, truth be told, the majority of the four hundred people who lived here didn't. But over the past few weeks her list had grown to a good number of people anyway, mostly the elderly, those with chronic illnesses and the children.

She looked at the modestly long line outside Mrs Begay's house—Joanna had commandeered Mrs Begay's front room for the clinic today. With a rickety card table and a metal folding chair, this was a much nicer arrangement than she'd had in Whitestone last week, where she'd been forced to set up on a sidewalk. Thank God it hardly ever rained in the Big Open, because she'd had to explain, almost with every shot she administered, what it was for and what it would do. It took hours, and in the rain it wouldn't have been much fun. Especially since every one of them asked for a detailed explanation, not because they didn't know what a flu vaccination was for—they did, since they got one every year there was a doctor on the reservation—but because Joanna still had to prove herself to them. Six months on this circuit, and she still wasn't as trusted as she'd hoped to be. The good people of Whitestone had merely been putting her to the test with their questions—trying to decide whether or not they liked her.

Whoever had said this was going to be easy?

First person in line was Billy Begay, age ten. Joanna had his chart, a sparse leftover from the last doctor. According to the two pages inside, nothing about Billy seemed unusual. Normal, healthy, somewhat over his ideal body weight. He'd had measles and chickenpox. That was it.

"OK, Billy, this is going to hurt a little. Just a pinch. Look the other way and when I count to three…" Of course, she jabbed him on the count of two.

"Can I have a sucker now, DocJo?" Billy asked. "A green one?"

Automatically, Joanna reached into her goody bag, but something stopped her before she handed the sucker over to Billy. Age ten, and he was pudgy. Too pudgy. Six months on the reservation had taught her to be cautious, since about a quarter of the children here were at risk for diabetes. So, instead of handing him the candy, she asked, "Do you get thirsty a lot?"

"Sometimes," he said, his eyes fixed squarely on the goody bag.

"Do you play outside with your friends very much?"

"Uh-uh. I like video games better. And TV."

"Hang on, Billy. I need to grab something real fast." That nagging feeling was turning into a warning siren now.

The youngest she'd seen with diabetes out here was six, and while diabetes at that age was unusual the statistics spoke volumes, and there was something about Billy that fit the profile. Grabbing a blood-sugar meter out of her medical bag, Joanna swabbed Billy's finger with an alcohol wipe, did a finger prick then counted off the seconds for the results. Thirty seconds later, sure enough, Billy's blood sugar was 240. "Oh, my God," she whispered. Twice the normal level. "When was the last time you ate something?" she asked him.

"At lunch, a few hours ago. Then I had some cookies afterward for a snack. And a root beer. So do I get my sucker now, or what?" He was getting impatient.

All the sugar in him could certainly raise his blood sugar level, but common sense told her Billy needed better testing. "Mrs Begay, does anyone in your family have diabetes?" she asked Billy's mom.

"My husband, but he takes care of it himself."

Joanna knew what that meant. He ignored it. That had been a constant battle for her since she'd been here, treating so many people like Billy's dad who "took care of it" on their own. "I need to test Billy for diabetes. His blood sugar's high, and he fits the profile."

"We'll take care of him, just like we do my husband," Mrs Begay said, smiling. "So if he can have his sucker now, we'll move along so you can get to the others."

"If he's diabetic he can't have a sucker, Mrs Begay," Joanna stated. "It'll make his blood sugar go even higher. Does your husband ever test himself?"

"With what?"

"Something like this?" Joanna held up her meter.

"No. We can't afford something like that. The doctors up in Fort Peck told Arthur he should, and they even gave him one to use, but we ran out of those strips that go in it, so we put it away."

"Then what does your husband do to take care of himself? Is he on medication? Pills? Shots?"

"No medicine. But he drinks diet soda now."

"And that's it?"

Mrs Begay nodded. "And he feels much better."

Joanna smiled. Of all the American Indians who received medical treatment from Indian Medical Alliances, for which she worked, about sixteen percent were diagnosed with diabetes. But on reservations such as Hawk, not even half the people received medical services, so who knew what she was looking at? Except right now she was looking at Billy Begay, who was too young to be going through this. "I need to come back in a few days and do some more tests on Billy so I can see for sure if he is, or isn't, diabetic."

"More blood?" Billy whined.

"Afraid so. But I'll bring you your very own case of diet soda then, since I can't give you the sucker now. How's that sound?"

He shrugged before he walked away. Apparently it didn't sound too good. But who could blame the kid? At thirty-three years old, Joanna still liked an occasional sucker herself. Like Billy, a green one.

Midnight, and she was finally home. Well, at least the place she called home when she wasn't home, which was an apartment in Billings. One barely furnished, and hardly ever used. But she did get a day off every once in a while and it was nice to go someplace other than where she worked. So technically, at this moment, she was home enough. And someone was sleeping in her bed, she suddenly remembered.

"Great," she muttered, plodding in the front door. "Dusty, tired and I don't even get to sleep in my own bed because *he's* there." She assumed he was there since his car, that impractical pile of nuts and bolts, was sitting out front. In her spot! Everybody in Rising Sun knew that was her spot directly in front of the clinic. But he was in it, which meant she'd had to park three spots away. Damn him!

Pulling off her boots and tossing them at the bottom step, she stomped up the stairs, taking particular care to make as much noise as she could. Since *he* wasn't there to work, no way was Dr Ducheneaux getting the bed while she was forced to make do with an examining table. No way in hell. "Get up," she yelled, once she reached the top step. "I want the bed, and I want it now!"

The room expanse on the second floor was quite open. No real room dividers but the sheets she'd hung. Just stairs leading to a loft-like structure. No doors, no privacy except in the bathroom, which was where she was headed for a quick shower. Then off to bed for six straight hours of sleep. "I'm going to take a shower, and I'll be out in five minutes. Since you're here to be a freeloader, I expect you to be downstairs when I get out. Use the examining table, or the floor, for all I care. Anything but my bed."

Sure, she wasn't being very hospitable, but the guy was here under false pretenses and he didn't deserve hospitable. He really didn't even deserve her roof over his head, except that her roof was owned by his grandmother. Apparently she'd bought it after the last doctor left, hoping that her grandson might come back to Hawk to practice. Poor lady couldn't have known her grandson too well.

Five minutes in the shower, then Joanna hopped out, dried off and decided to braid her hair instead of drying it. Drying took too much effort and braiding kept it neat enough. So she wound it into a braid that dropped just below her shoulders—red braid, so unlike all the black braids she was used to seeing—wrapped herself in a towel and wandered out to the crude pine armoire that held her clothes. Normally she slept in shorts and T-shirt—simple and cool enough. And modest, since there had been more than one time when someone had come knocking on her door in the middle of the night. Glancing over her shoulder, she saw that her bed was empty. Rumpled, definitely slept in, and void of human life at the moment. At least he'd had the decency to surrender it to her.

She dropped the towel, and bent down to put on her panties. Skimpies for sure, definitely on the cheeky side, but not quite a thong, they were basic white and cotton. A real practicality for the Montana desert lands.

"Can't say I've had a greeting like that in a while," he said from the top of the stairs.

Pulling up her panties and trying not to trip herself up doing so, Joanna spun around to him, realized that she was bare-breasted, and crossed her arms over her chest. "What are you doing up here?" she shrieked.

"Going to bed, I thought. Are you joining me?"

The look on his face was insufferably amused. Even in the dim light she was afforded in her living quarters she could see that. She could also see that he was giving her the once-over. "I told you I was taking the bed, that you could have the examining table." She wanted to move, wanted to grab something to cover herself, but to that she'd first have to let him have a better look than he'd already had, and she wasn't about to do that.

"Last thing I recall is that you said I'd have to make my own damned bed. Which I did, as you can see. Then I took a nap in it."

"Five minutes ago, Doctor. When I came in, I told you to—"

"Five minutes ago I was saying goodnight to my grandmother."

"Would you go downstairs so I can get dressed?"

"Too late, Jo, I've seen it all."

"Joanna," she snapped.

"Excuse me. I've seen it all, *Joanna*. But since we're

both doctors here, it doesn't matter. At least not to me. Very nice, though!''

Bare-breasted or not, Joanna dropped her modest pose, grabbed the nearest thing she could find, a weighty volume on wilderness emergency medicine, and heaved it at him. ''Get out,'' she yelled.

Laughing, Chay turned and dashed down the stairs. At the bottom he turned and looked back up but she wasn't in sight. ''Thank you,'' he called. ''It was a pleasure.''

Pulling on her shirt and shorts, Joanna dived into her bed and yanked the sheet up to her chin. Normally on hot Montana nights such as this she slept without a cover. But not tonight, not with Chayton Ducheneaux in the house.

The examining table wasn't comfortable, neither was it nearly long enough for him, so Chayton made a reasonably passable bed on the floor in the tiny room Joanna used as an office, pulled off his khakis and polo shirt, and lay down on top of the bedding. He'd spent a pleasant couple of hours with his grandmother. He called her sometimes, as he did his mother, and sent her gifts and cards on appropriate occasions. She'd been anxious to hear about his life in the big city, his medical practice, his friends…his girlfriend. She made a particular point of bringing that up, and showed the appropriate amount of disappointment when he'd told her he was hopelessly alone. ''Then what do you do with all your time?'' she'd asked. ''Since you're not spending it with a woman? It's not a man, is it? You're not keeping company with men these days, are you?''

''Not a man,'' he'd told her. ''I just don't have much time.'' At thirty-six, he was on the fast track to becoming the chief of orthopedic services. That meant lots of hours, but he wanted it so badly nothing else mattered, and nothing else in his life came first. Including women. Sure, he dated every now and then, occasionally had a little fling that progressed beyond a simple date. But once or twice with a woman and the brakes went on. It was too risky, and at his place in life he didn't want risk.

At least Macawi had been glad to hear that when he did find time for a social life, it was with a woman. That gave her some hope for the Ducheneaux great-grandchild she wanted. "You're the only Ducheneaux," she'd told him. "The only one to carry the family name." Except his father had said he brought dishonor to the name.

One son, no other children, and he was a disappointment. Sighing, Chay turned over on his side and closed his eyes. But as he did so, the image that filled his head wasn't about disappointments or family obligations. Those would have been far easier because he was used to them. This image, though…well, it sure wasn't going to let him sleep any time soon. Not with Joanna Killian, buck naked and drop-dead beautiful, jumping out at him as soon as his eyelids fluttered down. *Anpaytoo*. Radiant. Definitely that, and so much more!

CHAPTER THREE

"PERSONALLY, I don't care if they see you in your boxers, but they might be offended."

"Huh?" Joanna's words cut through Chay's sleep but not so much that he could attach any significant meaning to them.

"And your feet are sticking out into the hall. I don't have insurance here so pull them in before somebody trips over them and falls."

More words, and he was finally beginning to wake up. Damn, he was stiff. He could feel it even before he opened his eyes. Stiff neck, stiff back. What in the world had he done to cause all that? he wondered as he finally braved the light streaming in from the... He opened his eyes, looked up, saw the overhead ceiling light. "What the hell?" he muttered, twisting his neck, only to find that he was wedged up tight against a desk and looking under it at...pink bunny slippers. Now it was coming back to him. "I don't suppose you'd happen to have a cup of coffee up there, would you?"

"I don't suppose you'd happen to have a bathrobe down there, would you? I've got patients coming any minute now and as much as I love a good-looking, mostly naked male body sprawled at my feet, I think most of the people around here might take it the wrong way."

Chay sat up, noticed she'd tossed a bath towel over his middle, and smiled. So she was a bit of a prude. That surprised him. But prudish could be fun. Standing, he purposely let the towel drop to the floor, then watched Joanna struggle to not look at him. "Did you sleep well?"

"Do you really care?" She was forcing herself to look at the desk top.

"No, but I thought since I was standing here in front of you practically naked, a little civility might be in order. Especially as last night, when you were standing in front of me practically naked, you weren't civil at all." She was actually blushing, he noticed. A hearty red flush was creeping up her neck and splotching its way across her cheeks. "And since we're living together now…"

"We're not living together," she snapped, finally looking up at him. Her eyes were fiery. Green, angry and boring straight into his. "And let's get one thing straight. You're here because your grandmother owns the building. I'm here because I'm the doctor. You can stay, but stay out of my way, and stay away from my patients. And for heaven's sake, put on some pants, will you, instead of standing there flaunting whatever it is you think you're flaunting at me? Because, for your information, Dr Ducheneaux, like you said last night, I've seen it all. And in this case, I'm not interested."

Damn, she was sexy when she was angry. Sexy, gorgeous, and cute in her bunnies. Not exactly what he was looking for on Hawk. "For your information, Dr Killian, I think the fact that you're so offended by me being here, practically naked, speaks for itself." He shot her his never-fail grin. The one that always melted them.

"And what's it saying, Doctor Ducheneaux?"

"That Dr Killian *is* interested." With that, he turned and headed up the stairs. Time to grab a quick shower and go see his mother. Even though, admittedly, he'd rather stay right where he was and see more of Joanna.

Joanna watched him saunter up the stairs. It was a deliberate saunter, she suspected. The man was in no particular hurry, and most likely he knew she was watching every step he took. Which she was, damn him! She might be laying off personal relationships for a while, but that didn't stop her from looking at him. And he was definitely worth looking at. Nothing that good in boxers had passed her way since…well, since ever. Including during her marriage.

When he was finally out of sight, Joanna glanced at the clock. Five minutes till six. Patients were probably waiting outside right now, too polite to knock on the door. If she didn't open up for another hour, they still wouldn't knock. That's how they were. Kind, uncomplaining. Unassuming. Never intrusive.

Kicking her bunnies into the corner, she slipped into some rubber-soled moccasins, hurried to the front door, unlocked it and pulled it open. Sure enough, there they were. At least thirty of them, standing in a tidy line extending down the sidewalk, waiting for her. A day's worth of patients when she had only half a day to give them.

"No, I'm not living with Dr Killian. Just sleeping under her desk." Chay reached over to the platter of buttermilk biscuits his mother had set in front of him and took his fourth. Lots of butter and it was pure heaven. There was nothing better for breakfast than his mom's biscuits, and he suddenly realized how much he'd missed them.

"So you're not going to tell me why you're here?" Wenona asked. The diner was bustling this morning. It always did, mostly with men on their way to work at the ranch.

"Do I have to have a reason to—" He'd almost said *come home*, but he'd caught himself in the nick of time. "To visit?"

"You haven't had a reason to visit in eight years so, yes, I think you do have to have a reason." She bustled over to the pick-up window, grabbed two platters full of sausages, bacon, eggs, fried potatoes and biscuits and took them to a booth at the far end of the room. Chay watched her, smiling. Nearly sixty, and she wasn't slowing down. It was as if time had stood still around his mother. But apparently not so with his dad. At least that's what his grandmother had told him last night. Leonard was looking old, she said. Old enough to be Wenona's father. He had deep wrinkles in his face now, walked too slowly, was too thin. Vague symptoms, and possibly just the effects of sixty-five years of hard work. Chay had promised Macawi he'd try and talk to his dad. It wouldn't do any good, because he was sure his dad wouldn't talk back.

"I had time off and decided I wanted to come see you since you refuse to come see me," he said as Wenona rushed back to the pick-up window for an order of pancakes.

"You may charm your way through Chicago, but not here, Chayton. Did Macawi ask you to come?" She sat the pancakes in front of a young man seated five spots away from Chayton, then refilled his coffee.

"She's worried," Chay conceded.

Wenona stopped in front of him, still holding the coffee-pot. "It's none of your concern. And if that's all you're here for, go home. Your father doesn't want your interference."

Chay cracked a bitter laugh. "As if I didn't know that."

"So why bother him, Chayton? You'll only upset him and aggravate yourself."

"Because my grandmother is worried and she asked me to do this for her."

"Your father doesn't believe in your kind of medicine."

How many times had they had that argument, he and his father? Theirs was a family of healers—shamans. Three generations before Chay. Chay's father was a healer, too. He wasn't a doctor, didn't have medical training. He stuck to the old ways, the spiritual methods that were more tradition than practical. Most Indians sought regular medicine in clinics and hospitals, but there were still a few holdouts, his dad being the biggest one of them all on Hawk Reservation. And the day Chay had announced that he was going to be a doctor had been the last day his father had ever spoken to him. *If you do then you're no son of mine.* And he hadn't been his dad's son for eighteen years now.

"For Macawi's sake I'm going to try. She knows how he is and she knows he probably won't see me, but I'm doing this for her, because she loves him and, unlike my father, she hasn't turned her back on her child. And I don't want that causing problems between you and me. OK?" He shot her his typical Chayton grin, then blew her a kiss. "OK?"

"I never could resist a good-looking man," she said.

"So can you take some time off, or am I going to have to sit here at the counter all day just to spend time with my mother?"

"This afternoon. I've asked Fern Holly Tree to cover for me and she'll be in right after the lunch rush is over."

"How is Fern?" He'd dated her daughter, Jane, before he'd gone off to community college. Jane Holly Tree…the memory brought a smile to his face. Happy, bubbly, always smiling. And in his opinion, the prettiest girl on Hawk. She might have been the one he would have taken with him except she'd chosen the traditional ways—had married a man who'd gone to work on the ranch, probably had lots of babies by now.

"Don't you mean how's Jane?" his mother asked.

"Her, too."

"Fern *and* Jane are fine. Fern retired from the school last year and Jane divorced her husband and moved to Seattle. She does something with computers now."

Chay raised his eyebrows. "Times change. Look, I'll be back after lunch and we can…" He wasn't sure what they could do since there wasn't anything to do in Rising Sun. "We can do anything you'd like to do this afternoon."

Standing, he bent over the counter, gave his mother a kiss on the cheek, then vacated the stool for the next hungry rancher coming through the door.

Outside, he looked up and down the street. Joanna's line had dwindled, but not much. No one seemed too sick, he thought. At least, not from his vantage point.

"You should go help her!"

Chay spun around to face his grandmother. Her arms were loaded with grocery sacks, and he reached to take them from him, but she jerked away from him. "I can carry these," she said, "and you can go be a doctor. That's the way it should be, Chayton. The way it's meant to be."

"How about I carry your bags home for you, then *think* about helping Joanna?" The wrong thing to say. His grandmother already had that devilish glint in her eyes. The one that, as a child, he'd come to recognize as her winning, him losing. Didn't matter what they were winning or losing. When he saw that glint he knew he was a goner. And if anything, it was sharper now than when she'd been younger. "You do realize I didn't come here to work, don't you?"

"We all work, Chayton. That's why we're put here. And that's a lesson I'm sure you haven't forgotten from the old days."

No escaping it. His grandmother was going to have her way and it was like all the years they'd been separated had vanished and they'd taken up where they'd left off when he'd been twenty-eight, or eighteen, or eight. "I've really missed you," he said, giving her an affectionate kiss on the forehead.

"And you should have," she said, thrusting her grocery bags at him.

Leaning against the doorframe of the examining room, arms crossed casually over his chest, one leg crossed casually over the other, Chay grinned at Joanna. "OK, I'm all yours for a couple of hours. Where do you want me?"

Joanna was about to remove stitches from an old-timer. Long hair hanging most of the way down his back and a big toothless grin, the man had a zigzag cut up his right forearm. "Gee, Doctor, isn't that generous of you?" Joanna retorted.

"I thought it was."

"If I weren't in desperate need of help, I'd tell you exactly where I'd like you to go, but I'm not in a position to turn down help, even if it's only yours. So you start right here with Bob Turning Bull. He took a fall, I stitched him up and now it's time for them to come out. Oh, and he has another more delicate complaint. One he doesn't want to discuss with a woman. Maybe you can get him to tell you about it."

She smiled as she hurried out of the room to see who was next in line. "And if you need any help, just give me a shout."

"I think I can handle stitches, *Joanna.*"

The way he'd said her name gave her a little chill. His voice was deep and seductive already, but the way *Joanna* had rolled off his tongue…She shivered again, just thinking about it. *OK, pull back here, Joanna. Focus. Avoid the distractions.* Not enough time, absolutely not enough energy to do otherwise. More than that, he was a doctor, for heaven's sake. What in the world was she thinking? She'd had one once and once was definitely enough. "It's not the stitches I'm worried about. Oh, and Mr Turning Bull is a little hard of hearing." That was putting it mildly.

Joanna took the next patient into the tiny examining room adjacent to the one where Chayton was about to have a meaningful experience with Bob Turning Bull. Finally, something that would brighten her hectic day. "So what can I do for you, Mrs One Feather?"

"Another headache. I take the pills you give me and the headaches go away, but they always seem to come back."

"Well, I may have just what you need." Joanna pulled a glasses case from her pocket. Reading glasses, not prescription. Alice One Feather was a seamstress who did all her tiny detail work by hand. Her headaches always came at the end of her work day, and since there were no other symptoms—no high blood pressure, visual distortion, slurred speech, neurological impairment—to go along with the headaches, the logical assumption seemed to be poor eyesight. Joanna hoped so, anyway, because there was no way Alice would submit to tests other than what was simple and convenient. She'd made that perfectly clear at her first visit to see Joanna. Fix the problem there, or skip it. She'd said it in a polite way, of course, but the response was the same thing she'd heard from a lot of other people on Hawk. Convenience, or nothing. Probably had something to do with the fact that many of the people here were still tottering on the verge of disbelief in Joanna's kind of medicine.

"I want you to use these when you do any close-up work—sewing, reading, anything to do with your eyes. If it's simple eye strain, they might help." So many ifs out here. If it's eye strain, if it's simple dermatitis, if it's a plain old belly ache. In a time when medicine was so advanced, Joanna was working fifty years in the past and keeping her fingers crossed every time she prescribed something.

Alice One Feather scrambled out of the room clutching her glasses, and as soon as she was out the door Joanna plopped herself down on top of the examining table for a couple of minutes just to give her feet and back a little break. Two minutes was all she could afford, then back to work.

"What kind of pain are you experiencing?" Chay said. The rooms had paper-thin walls and anything above a normal tone of voice was fair game for anyone who cared to listen. Luckily, the people still in the waiting room, at least ten of them, were chatting, in effect acting as a privacy barrier to the voice level Chay was going to have to use in order to be heard by Mr Turning Bull. "I said, what kind of pain are you experiencing?" This time his voice was a little louder.

Joanna smiled. Not quite there yet, but he was getting closer.

"Where's your pain, Mr Turning Bull? Where do you hurt?"

Yep, loud enough to be heard this time. Joanna hopped off the table and wandered into Chayton's exam room. "Need some help?"

"No, I don't need help," he snapped. "It's abdominal pain. I can figure it out."

"Suit yourself." She stepped back out, shut the door, and returned to the examining table for another few minutes off her feet, thanks to Bob Turning Bull. He deserved his privacy, and having another patient back in the examining area certainly wouldn't give him any. Not even through closed doors. So she hopped back up on the table, lay back and closed her eyes. *Take the breaks any way you can get them, Joanna.* They didn't happen too often.

Chay poked and probed Bob Turning Bull's belly for a good five minutes, eliciting absolutely no reaction from him. Except for the fact that his belly was a little rigid and distended, there didn't seem to be much the matter with him. Still, Chay wasn't ready to give him a dose of some generic stomach medicine and send him on his way. Not when the thought of bowel obstruction kept popping into his mind. Bowel obstruction. The man was close to eighty. That could easily happen. But what did Chay know about bowel obstructions? He was an orthopedist, for heaven's sake. He fixed bones, not guts. "Have you been passing any gas?" It seemed like the logical question to ask, he thought.

"What?"

"Gas, Mr Turning Bull. Have you been passing any gas?" he repeated, this time louder.

"What?" Bob Turning Bull's voice seemed to rise in direct proportion to Chay's.

"Have you been expelling any gas? *Gas*. Are you expelling gas?" By now everybody out on the street was probably hearing him. For sure, everybody in the waiting room was privy to Mr Turning Bull's delicate condition. "Do you have gas, Mr Turning Bull?" he shouted.

Bob Turning Bull drew himself up in an indignant stance and shouted, "No, sir. That certainly wasn't me! Must have been you expelling gas, Doctor, because I surely did no such thing."

The waiting room erupted in laughter. So did Joanna, from the hall. Poking her head into the room, she wasn't even trying to keep a straight face. "Here, have him take this home." She tossed him a boxed enema.

"You set me up, didn't you?" Chay said. "I thought you said he wouldn't talk to you about his complaint."

"He won't, Doctor. But that doesn't mean I don't know what it is." Grinning, she backed out and shut the door, leaving Chay there with an old man who was giving him an irate, if not disgusted look.

"You ought to be ashamed of yourself, young man," Bob Turning Bull yelled, heading to the door. "People your age should know better." He shook his head in distaste. "Shame on you." Then he ambled away, glancing back to give Chay one more disgusted look before he turned the corner into the waiting room.

"Ready for your next one?" Joanna asked, not even trying to hide her grin. She was leaning against the hall wall, arms crossed casually against her chest, one leg crossed casually over the other—mimicking his stance from earlier, grinning for all she was worth.

"No, I'm not ready for the next one." He noticed that Joanna's nose wrinkled when she smiled. Cute wrinkle. Cute nose. Too cute to punch, which was what she deserved for pulling that last stunt on him. Actually, rather than punching, he felt more like kissing that nose. *Whoa, Chay. Where the hell did that come from?*

See his dad, get rejected one more time then get the hell out of Rising Sun and off the Hawk Reservation. That was it, and Joanna and her cute little nose didn't fit into that plan anywhere.

"OK. So maybe it was a little mean of me to stick Mr Turning Bull on you like that, but all I can say is welcome to my world, Chayton."

"Chay."

"Chay. Just thought I'd give you the crash course in circuit medicine in the Big Open."

"Don't you mean more like crash and burn in the Big Open?" He chuckled. "I think one patient was enough. Not sure I'm up to another one."

"Well, I'll take Mrs Bassett, who's next up, but in case you change your mind, the one after her's a piece of cake. Sweet lady who has a little gout. She takes an anti-inflammatory for it, and she comes in once a week pretty much for no reason other than some reassurance. Her name's Ivy Lebeau."

"Mrs Lebeau?" Ivy Swiftbird Lebeau had been his grade school teacher. He'd endured six years in a one-room school that took in a mixture of grade levels, and Mrs Lebeau was an extraordinary teacher under the worst of circumstances.

Joanna nodded. "And since you're an orthopod, maybe that's a little closer to what you do."

"What does she take?"

"Ibuprofen."

"Any dietary adjustments?" Gout, unlike other forms of arthritis, is often triggered by dietary habits—not necessarily poor dietary habits but excesses in foods like red meat, and especially the organ meats. If there was one thing in abundance on Hawk, it was red meat. Gout's worst enemy in many cases.

"She gave up shellfish." Joanna grinned. "Although I don't think she's ever eaten it. But she was willing to give it up."

"Let me see what I can do. She's not hard of hearing, is she?"

"Sharp as a tack with perfect hearing."

Joanna went to greet her next patient while Chay hesitated outside the examination room in which Mrs Lebeau was waiting. Admittedly, he was a little nervous. This was not the impersonal situation he was used to. Inside was a person who'd made a tremendous difference in his life and he didn't know what to expect from her. "Hello, Mrs Lebeau," he said, finally stepping in.

"Macawi told me you were back," she snorted. "It's about time, running off the way you did, Chayton!"

Joanna had called her sweet? Chay smiled patiently. Apparently, Mrs Lebeau was another of the many who weren't too happy to see him. He was disappointed by her reaction, but he could deal with it. "I understand you have a little gout."

"Not a little, Chayton. If you understood all the details of gout, and I'm assuming that you do since you are an orthopedic specialist, then you'd know that there's no such thing as *a little* gout. I should have thought they would teach you better in medical school."

Same old Mrs Lebeau. Tiny, barely five feet and ninety pounds and exacting, abrasive, no-nonsense. And probably the reason he was a doctor today, although he'd never tell her that. Like everybody else, her plans had been for him to go to community college, get that degree in agriculture, then come back to the reservation. "What I know is that you're still eating red meat. Probably beans too, and lentils and peas."

She held up her right foot to show him her inflamed big toe. Red skin, warm to the touch. "I've cut my portions back and given up the organ meats, except kidney. I do like a good kidney stew every once in a while."

"Are you drinking more water? Water washes out the acids that cause gout—"

"Of course I'm drinking more water. I'm not an idiot, young man, and I don't appreciate you taking that attitude with me. I understand what the water does and I drink as much as Dr Killian told me to do. And I'm staying off my feet more. Your father came to see me last week and told me to walk with a cane, so I'm doing that, too."

His father. The healer. Even Mrs Lebeau, who was educated, still clung to some of the old ways, and that wasn't going to change. "Would you consider taking a different drug?"

"No."

"An injection in your toe?"

"Absolutely not, Chayton. And don't even suggest such a thing to me again."

His patience was beginning to wear thin. She came for treatment, but refused it. "Will you limit kidney stew to once a month?"

"Yes, I'm willing to do that."

Now he was getting somewhere. "Cut out the beans."

"Beans once a week, and that's not negotiable."

Beans were an inexpensive and easy staple. Cutting them out entirely would probably be a financial hardship to Mrs Lebeau. "I can live with that," he said, chuckling. This was the first time in his medical career that a patient's treatment had boiled down to roll-up-the-sleeves negotiation. "But you've got to cut your red meat consumption in half and eat more chicken or turkey. That's the only way I'll accept *any* beans.''

Teetering on the edge of the examining table, with her feet resting on the pull-out footrest, Ivy Lebeau crooked her finger at Chayton. ''Come here,'' she said.

He remembered that finger, that summons. Sometimes it had been good, most often it had been the invitation to go stand in the corner. He obliged, then bent down to her as she motioned him to do so.

''You're a good boy, Chayton. It's nice that you finally came home.'' Then she patted him on the cheek. ''I'll eat chicken and turkey if that makes you happy.''

Chay was helping Mrs Lebeau to the door when Joanna rushed in, breathless. ''I have a patient out in Steele. He's been laid up with a fractured femur. Hairline, not serious at the time of diagnosis. His mother just called and she thinks Michael has re-broken his leg. He's eight. She says it's swelling up pretty badly, a lot worse than it did the first time, and this time he's having trouble breathing!''

Immediately Chay jumped way ahead of Joanna's information to the possibilities. Blood loss from the bone, blood-vessel damage, nerve damage. Amputation. ''How long will it take me to get there?''

CHAPTER FOUR

THE drive to Steele was normally half an hour for Joanna when she was taking her time, but she could cut ten minutes off of that if she had to—another five if the emergency was life-threatening. Michael Red Elk's emergency lay somewhere in the realm where ten to fifteen minutes chopped off was mandatory. "I saw him yesterday, gave him permission to resume some activity."

"Follow-up X-ray?" Chay asked.

"I was lucky to get the diagnostic X-ray when he broke his leg. Follow-ups of any sort don't usually happen out here." No one was on the road. Good thing, with her speed exceeding the limit by half as much again. One of the good things about living in the Big Open was that it was just that. Big and open. There was no one else around, no one to get in her way in times such as this. "I always ask, but most of the time I get turned down."

"Do you have your own X-ray machine?"

Joanna laughed. "You're kidding me, right? You saw what I have, and there's no X-ray machine there."

"I thought maybe one of your other clinics—"

"My other clinics are the buildings *du jour* that I can grab. Yesterday it was Mrs Begay's living room. Last week it was the sidewalk. No clinics, Chay. Rising Sun is as modern as medicine gets out here." Although she'd become the queen of scrounging, always begging at the hospital door for anything they were going to toss into the trash. She had a twenty-years-outdated EKG machine, and it still worked well enough. Plus a defibrillator. All fit for the big city hospital trash piles, but in her clinic they were welcome additions. And, yes, she had the word out at hospitals all over Montana that she was looking for X-ray equipment. Even an old portable would be good. So far, though, no luck.

"I guess I never realized how bad it is." He slid down into the passenger's seat next to Joanna and stared off to the side of the road. "When you're a kid it is what it is. Not good, not bad. Just what it is."

"So why'd you leave?"

"A lot of reasons. Living out in the world gave me more perspectives than I realized any one man was allowed to have here. For the first time in my life I was free—no restrictions, no expectations, no obligations. Growing up as the son of one of the tribal leaders, there are always a lot of expectations. The ones everybody had for me didn't fit with the ones I had for myself, so when I left, I left."

"Did you ever look back?"

"All the time. Everything Hawk is, and isn't, is a part of me. Only thing is, I could look, but I couldn't come back. It had to be all or nothing. So, why did *you* strand yourself out here? By choice, or did someone banish you from somewhere?" He chuckled. "Any deep, dark secrets you want to reveal?"

She glanced over at him. He was so casual, such a good fit out here. Not like her, always trying to fit in someplace...any place. "Not deep, not dark and definitely not a secret. I just got divorced. He took the practice, I hit the road." Simple enough. No need to mention differing expectations and needs and outlooks. Those were a year in her past now and, like Chay, sometimes she looked back, but she wouldn't go back.

"And so you ended up here, at the end of the road."

"Or the beginning, depending on what you want."

They were sailing by the cattle ranch and she noticed Chay deliberately turn his head away. She knew the story. At least the cursory details of it. Everybody did. The good son gone bad. Or, in Chay's case, gone away, never to return, which was the same thing as gone bad. Pity. Leonard Ducheneaux was a nice man. He had his stubborn ways, but he was a decent, hard worker who apparently had an iron resolve when it came to his son. *No son*, he would say.

Sadly, he meant it.

"Have you seen my father lately?" Chay asked.

That surprised her a little. Somehow she'd assumed Chay would be as stubborn as his father. *No father.* "In passing. Why?"

"Not as a patient?"

"If I had…"

"Yeah, yeah. I know. You couldn't tell me."

"But since I haven't, I guess it doesn't matter, does it?"

He glanced over at the ranch. Just a quick glance at pretty much nothing now. They were long past the headquarters building and the bunkhouses where those who didn't make it home every night slept. Right now the only scenery was wide open prairie. "I'm assuming you know how it is between my father and me? Not many secrets."

"I've heard some things."

"I'll just bet you have." He laughed bitterly. "A mass murderer would be more welcome here than I am." He glanced over at the ranch again. "So is this what you really want, Joanna?"

"What I really want is all this with a nice, new, modern medical clinic to go along with it."

"And you're the crusader who's going to build it?"

"Is that cynicism I'm hearing in your voice?" she asked. "The doctor from Chicago doesn't think I can do it?" Of course he didn't. It was silly to waste good breath even mentioning it. Living the hard life, fighting the hard battles wasn't part of the medical repertoire any more. At least in Chay's medical circles. Thank God she never crossed over into his medical circles.

"Yes. I've seen it happen too many times. A do-gooder comes in, raises the hopes of the people with empty and probably well-meant promises, then leaves once he, or she, realizes just how empty those promises were. And I don't doubt that you mean it when you say you want to set up a nice new, modern clinic out here. I'm sure you do. But so did the doctor before you, and the doctor before that. So, yes, that's cynicism you're hearing because I'm a cynic. I was born and raised here, and if there's one thing I've never done it's delude myself. Dreams don't happen out here. So I admire your ambitions and wish you well with them, but don't count me among the optimists, because I'm not."

"And this is where you expect me to get offended and huffy and defensive, and tell you how wrong you are, that I can do anything I set my mind to?" Truth was, she wasn't offended. Chay was right on most counts, except one. Dreams could happen anywhere. She believed it, had always believed it, and in the dark hours, when she was too exhausted to crawl up her stairs to bed, and curling up on the floor at the bottom of them was good enough, she still had that dream.

"Can you?"

"What?"

"Do anything you set your mind to?"

"I suppose if you stay here long enough, you'll be able to see for yourself."

There was a small crowd gathered outside Betty Red Elk's house. Mostly women, a few children. They were unusually quiet. Not a good sign, she thought. These people were outgoing, gregarious, and even before she stopped her Jeep she could see worried expressions all around. "I think it's bad," she said, grabbing her medical bag.

"What kind of doctor are you, Joanna?"

"Now you ask?"

"Just wanted to know what I was getting myself into. I

mean, I've assumed you're a medical doctor, but for all I know you could be a proctologist, which won't do this poor kid any good at all unless it turns out to be a hemorrhoid instead of a broken leg."

"Internal medicine. Which means I can hold my own with a hemorrhoid. But I've had training in trauma, so I'm not too bad with a broken leg either."

The crowd parted as Joanna and Chay made their way up to the front door, and the first thing she noticed as she pulled the screen door back was that it was too quiet inside the house. Michael should have been sobbing, maybe screaming, but there was nothing. Not a peep. Not from Michael, not from his mother.

Joanna knew the way to the bedroom occupied by all four of the Red Elk sons and hurried along the darkened hallway to the tiny eight-by-ten room where she saw Michael lying on the bottom bunk of the two bunk beds lining the walls. Fred and Betty Red Elk were huddling near the closet door opposite the beds while Leonard Ducheneaux was standing over the boy, saying words that Joanna didn't understand but knew to be a prayer of some sort. Michael needed more than prayers. But when it came to her healing versus Leonard Ducheneaux's, she was standing on the far side of a very thin line. One that she wasn't necessarily allowed to cross over, and when she was, the gesture was more often than not conditional.

"What's he doing?" she whispered to Chay.

"Not enough," he whispered, backing out of the room.

This wasn't the way he'd wanted it to be. Their first meeting in all these years shouldn't have been as healer to healer, one vying against the other for the treatment of a little boy. But that's what it had come down to. His father was going through the ritual of extraction—removing bad energy, replacing it with healing energy—but Chay needed to tend the boy's fracture, stabilizing his vital signs and finding a way to get him the hell out of there to a hospital. Time was precious here, but as he watched his father take the bad energy and neutralize it in a bowl of water, he knew there was no consideration of time in Leonard's practices. It was all about preparing the body spiritually to accept healing energy and not about treating the injury.

"Does this happen a lot?" he snapped at Joanna, who had stepped out of the cramped bedroom.

"Not a lot, but I run into it every now and then. They trust your father, and as often as not they call him before they call me."

"The kid could lose his leg."

"So what do you want me to do, Chay? Physically drag your father out of there? Because, apart from that, he's not going anywhere until he's finished."

Chay swiped angrily at his hair. "What kind of transport can we get to the nearest hospital in Billings? A helicopter?"

Joanna shook her head. "An ambulance maybe. Fastest way is to put Michael in his dad's truck and take him there straight away."

"Won't work. I don't want him on the road that long. Too bumpy. He's already shocky, and heaven knows what else is going on with him since I can't get close enough to take a look." He could hear his father chanting to the sun to come down and take the boy's pain into the water. Morphine would have been better.

"We only get a helicopter if it's life and death, since these people don't have insurance to pay for it."

"How about life and limb? Because that kid could lose his leg if it's what I think it is." Possibly a compartmental fracture, meaning the swelling was shutting off the circulation. Very bad, possibly even fatal in extreme cases.

"Unless you've got a credit card that hasn't blown over its limit, it's not going to happen. My superiors won't approve it."

"Yeah, well, watch me. Where the hell's the phone?"

"Do you know how much it's going to cost you?"

"Do you know what it's like to be eight and get your leg chopped off?" He paused, took a deep breath. "Go get Michael's vitals. The extraction's almost over. By now my father is filling the void where the bad energy was with a new healing energy, and he won't quit, or even be distracted, until that's done, so you won't be intruding."

"You know the ceremony?"

Hell, yes, he knew the ceremony. He'd gone through it with his father dozens of times. It was the only proper thing to do as the next shaman in the family lineage, to learn early the ways of his forefathers. In his case, that had happened when he'd been sixteen. "What's the matter? You don't recognize an honest-to-goodness shaman when you see one?" he muttered. "Look, I'll be back in a minute."

He found the phone on the kitchen wall, made a couple of calls, and offered up his credit-card number. As he was reciting the expiration date to the woman who was taking the information, the chopper had already been dispatched and was *en route*. "Wonder what my father would say about the healing energy in plastic?" he muttered, tucking the card back into his wallet.

Heading back to the hall, Chayton saw his father coming toward him. And Macawi was right. He looked old, tired. Too thin. All these years, and Chayton suddenly found himself with nothing to say. Which, as it turned out, didn't matter since his father didn't speak to him, didn't even glance his way, not for a fraction of a second, as he passed by. It was as it had been for a long time. To Leonard Ducheneaux, Chayton Ducheneaux did not exist.

Joanna saw the brief exchange. Lack of exchange was more like it. For a second she also thought she saw a flash of anguish cross Chay's face. *So he's not so cold-hearted after all*, she thought. It had to hurt him, even though he put up a good front. She remembered all the hurt from her own father. Two years when he'd preferred the bottle over her. Two years when she'd been turned away every time she'd tried approaching him. Yes, it hurt, and it was a pain she'd never get over because her father had died still turned away from her.

"Vitals normal," she said. "On the high side, but not bad. "Breathing is fine, too."

Chay brushed by her to Michael's bedside, and bent down to look at the leg. "How're you doing, Michael?" he asked, running his fingers lightly over the injury.

"I didn't mean to do it," he said. "But I thought it would be OK just for a couple of minutes."

"Football?" Joanna asked.

He didn't answer, but she could tell from the guilt crossing his face it had been football. Amazing, she thought, his lack of pain. Poor kid should have been in agony.

"It's definitely compartmental," Chay said, confirming his worst fears after he'd had a look. "I'm getting a tight feel to the muscle compartment. And Michael's sensation seems decreased overall."

Joanna sucked in her breath and held it. She'd never seen a compartmental fracture, but she certainly knew the consequences. Chay was right about this. Without speedy help Michael could—and probably would—lose his leg.

"How long ago did this happen?" he asked.

"This morning, early," Betty Red Elk responded. "Maybe six hours ago. We put his leg on some pillows, wrapped a bandage on it to keep the swelling down. Then we called…um…Leonard, and DocJo, of course."

"Damn. Almost too many hours. Look, I've called for a helicopter because Michael needs to go to the hospital. Mr

Red Elk, would you wait outside to watch for them? And, Mrs Red Elk, since Michael's going to need surgery this time, maybe you should go pack a few things for him.''

Both obliged quickly. ''What's up?'' Joanna asked.

Chay pulled her to the opposite side of the room from Michael. ''Six hours is still in safe territory if the swelling isn't too severe, but the limb has to stay flat and free of anything binding.''

''Oh, God,'' she moaned. ''They had his leg…'' She looked over at Michael.

''I need to do a fasciotomy to relieve the pressure before we can send him. Anything else is going to be risky, and that's the only way I can guarantee to save his leg.'' A fasciotomy was the removal of the fascia, thin connective tissue covering, or separating, the muscles and internal organs of the body. It was a simple procedure, but not one done in the field too often. Certainly, in her trauma experience Joanna had never done one. But she understood the need. Michael's hours were ticking away. His leg had already been elevated, which was the second worst thing that could have happened. The leg needed to stay level with the heart so it wouldn't strain so much to pump blood to it. And the worst thing had been wrapping it, keeping the swelling compressed. That put more pressure on the blood vessels and nerves. Combined, those two scenarios were serious, and poor Michael had been subjected to both. But an emergency fasciotomy here?

''You think he really needs it right now?'' she sputtered.

''He's your patient, Joanna, so it's your call. It could go either way. I might be wrong and he'll be fine until he can get to the hospital and have surgery. Or I might be right and he's on the verge of permanent and irreversible damage. But I'm only the hands here. You're his real doctor.''

She looked over at Michael, who was drifting off to sleep. ''Why's he doing that? Sleeping, staying calm, not acting like he's in pain,'' she asked. ''Did your dad do something? Give him something? Maybe some peyote? I've heard they, the healers, use peyote.'' A hallucinogenic made from the Peyote cactus.

Chay chuckled. ''He gave him some peace of mind maybe, but no drugs. Peyote is what my father uses to stay in touch with the spirits, but he wouldn't give it to someone else.''

''So that extraction thing he did might be working?'' Certainly, she didn't rule out the possibility. Having lived on the Hawk Reservation for six months now, she'd seen many medical situations that hadn't come with logical explanations. If Leonard's extraction ritual had given Michael the psychological or emotional boost to get through this, she'd thank Leonard next time she bumped into him.

''Maybe, maybe not. If he's a believer, then I suppose it worked.''

No way to tell if Chay was a believer. He was definitely an evader, but beyond that she didn't know. ''What's the helicopter's ETA?''

''Thirty minutes, then we're looking at another ten in preparation to transport, thirty back and at a minimum another thirty on top of that to get him prepped and into surgery.''

The time factor was certainly going against them at this point. ''Are you a good doctor, Chay?'' she asked. ''Your grandmother says you are, but she's your grandmother. I need to hear it from you. Are you good?'' He seemed like he was, and she wanted to believe that. But she didn't know. And the bottom line here was that she was risking Michael's leg to someone about whom she had questions.

He nodded, but said nothing.

Drawing in a deep breath, Joanna shut her eyes. Something deep inside was compelling her to trust him. Normally she wasn't like that. She wanted to see the proof—the outcome of other such surgeries, the credentials, the notes of his follow-ups. But he'd said he was good and for the first time in her practical, conservative life, something far beyond her normal logic was telling her to believe that he was good, and that he would save Michael's leg.

"So let's do it. I've got some minor surgical supplies in my bag, enough for a fasciotomy anyway. Plus Xylocaine if you want to give him a local anesthetic, morphine if you want something stronger. You tell me what to do."

"I'll prep him while you go explain it to his parents. OK?"

Joanna scurried down the hall to find Betty Red Elk, who was sitting in an old recliner. Clutching a backpack full of Michael's clothing and wringing it between her fingers, she was pale, shaking, on the verge of tears. Looking plaintively through the window at her husband standing out in the front yard waiting for the helicopter, then at Joanna, she asked, "Is he going to die, DocJo? Is my Michael going to die? I heard what you were talking about in there, about operating on him right here before you take him to Billings, and that sounds very serious."

Joanna bent down to her and took her hands. They were cold. But they would be. She was suffering the pain only a mother could feel when her child was so ill. "Dr Ducheneaux will take care of him."

"Ducheneaux?"

"Yes. He's Leonard's son, Chayton."

"I went to school with Chayton. I was a couple of years ahead of him so we were never friends, but I remember how he was different from the others around here. A lot like Michael is, always doing what he's not supposed to do even though he knows better."

A knot was forming in Joanna's gut. Would Betty have the sentiment of so many others, that Chay was no longer one of them, that he was to be shunned? The sentiment his own father held? If that turned out to be the case, and if Betty, or her husband, refused the emergency procedure because it was being done by Chay, Michael stood to lose his leg. Chay believed that to be the outcome. Because he did, so did she. "He's a very good doctor, Betty. A respected orthopedic surgeon in Chicago. Michael needs this surgery right now to save his leg and Chay has done it dozens of times. And I'm not qualified to do it, not the way Chay is." She sounded confident to her own ears, and she surely hoped that was coming across to Betty Red Elk, because if it wasn't…well, she didn't want to think about that. Michael was going to recover, and she was going to entrust that to Chay.

"When Leonard came to do the extraction, he said he was preparing Michael for the one who came after. I thought that meant you, DocJo, but it was Chayton, wasn't it?" She paused for a moment, looking to the hallway leading to Michael's room, even though Michael wasn't visible to her. "So, yes, I trust him to look after my boy the right way, whatever that is."

Relieved, Joanna took a couple of minutes to explain the procedure to the Red Elks, had them sign a consent form, then rushed back to the bedroom, where Michael was already prepped, and Chay was waiting at the side of the bed. She glanced at Michael, who was sound asleep. There was no fear on his face. No pain either. Nothing but the quiet look of a little boy who'd merely drifted off to dream little-boy dreams.

"So let's do it," Chay said. "I'll make the cut, you be the anesthesiologist, although I doubt he'll be waking up. If he does, I think two and a half of morphine will do him."

The procedure was quick. A swift, vertical incision over the swollen area of Michael's leg, a cut through the fatty tissue, none of it necrotic yet, Joanna noted as she looked over Chay's shoulder. That was good. The area wasn't yet dying for lack of blood flow.

Once he was through the fatty tissue, Chay excised a small piece of the fascia, then he swabbed the area with sterile gauze, bandaged it, and the procedure was over. Minimal bleeding, all things considered. And from the looks of it, minimal effort for Chay. He was so confident, Joanna thought. Certainly, with her experience in trauma she could have done this. But not the way he'd done it, not with such skill and precision. "Thank you," she said, pulling off her surgical gloves. "That was amazing."

Chay snapped off his own gloves and tossed them into the trash can. "What's amazing is that Betty Red Elk would even let me touch her son after my father was here." He took Joanna's stethoscope and placed it in his ears, then listened to Michael's chest. "Good heartbeat. Will you grab his BP?"

"Your father told her he was preparing Michael for the one who came after." Joanna slipped the cuff over Michael's arm, took the stethoscope from Chay, stuck it in her own ears and listened. "One-fifteen over seventy-five. Perfect!"

"Meaning you."

Joanna glanced at Chay sitting casually next to the bed now, as if this were an ordinary visit between two friends. Hawk Reservation needed Chay. And deep down she had the feeling that Chay needed Hawk. But the reconciliation was going to be a tough one, if there was to be a reconciliation at all. "Meaning you, Chay. You were the one who came after, and your father realized that."

"My father realizes nothing about me," he said, his voice unusually calm for such a pronouncement.

Many years of practicing avoidance and distance, Joanna decided. And many years of pain.

CHAPTER FIVE

"HE'S doing fine. Surgery fixed the fracture, no circulatory compromise, so he'll be up and about in a few weeks, so long as he stays away from football for a few months." It was after midnight now and Chay was tired to the bone. First the helicopter ride in to Billings, then hanging around with the Red Elks during Michael's surgery and staying afterward while Michael was still in Recovery had completely wiped him out. Sure, he was used to working long hours. He did it all the time, in fact. But not long hours with such high drama, and his wipeout was as much emotional as physical.

The ride back to Rising Sun with Fred Red Elk didn't help matters either. Fred wanted to talk, wanted reassurances about Michael, when all Chay wanted to do was sleep. Actually, he'd planned on crashing in an on-call room somewhere in the hospital and catching a ride back to Rising Sun in the morning, but Fred had to get back in order to show up for work at the ranch bright and early in the morning, so Chay had ridden along for moral support. As it turned out, Fred was one of Leonard's foremen—a responsible position he took seriously. So seriously, in fact, that he left his wife at the hospital with Michael and would drive that three-hundred-mile round trip tomorrow evening, and every other day it would be necessary, to spend a few minutes with the two of them. Most men would have called off work for a day or two, Chay thought. But the men out here didn't do that. Even under dire circumstances, such as a sick little boy, doing something like that probably never crossed their minds.

"How long are they going to keep him?" Joanna asked as Chay nearly staggered through the front door to the clinic.

"About a week, since he's still at risk of infection. I think they'd like to do some physical therapy—I know that's what I ordered. But the Red Elks wouldn't talk about it."

"Because the Red Elks can't afford it, and there's no place remotely close to here where Michael could get it even if they did have the money." She handed him a slice of hot pizza as he dropped down into the first chair he came to. "I've got some PT references. I'll read up and see what I can do for him."

Why did she do this to herself? he wondered. Hard, hard work, practically no pay, lousy hours, even lousier working conditions. And she was about to take on something that wasn't even close to her normal duties. "Have you ever considered doing something else?" he asked, stretching back, kicking his boots up on the chair across from him and relaxing for the first time in hours. "Maybe trying another kind of medicine?"

"Always wanted to be a ballet dancer, but I can't dance."

"Seriously. Have you ever thought about switching?"

"Seriously, no. I was raised in a place like this, Chay, only in West Virginia. Dirt-poor people, no jobs, no money, no health care. My mom died of pneumonia when I was seven because she couldn't afford to go to the doctor. My dad drank himself to death two years later because he didn't care enough to live. I think, for as long as I can remember, I always wanted to be someone who helped. And it's not about the money or the working conditions. It's about doing whatever I can do. You know, making a difference."

"I like to think that I make a difference in my practice." And he didn't have to make all the sacrifices to do it that Joanna did.

"Sure, you make a difference, and, please, don't take this the wrong way, but if you walked away from it tomorrow, one of your partners would take over for you, or they'd hire someone else. If I walked away from here tomorrow, these people would have no one. Did you know that it took nearly eighteen months to fill the last vacant position here? The last doctor quit a year and a half before I got here, Chay. Sure, there's always help over in Billings, or up in Fort Peck, but that's a long way away for someone like Michael who has a compartment injury and might lose his leg for a lack of getting to that help in time." She shrugged. "We live in different worlds, and there's nothing wrong with either one of them. People in Chicago need you the way you are, and people here need me the way I am."

"Are you happy here?"

"Happier than I've ever been anywhere else."

He shook his head. "Can't say that I understand it, but I admire your dedication."

"Well, my dedication's going to take me on the road for the next couple of days, so I need to call it a night and grab a few hours of sleep. I've set up a cot down here for me, so you can have the bed tonight. Since I'll probably be up earlier than you are, let me just say that it's been interesting meeting you, Dr Ducheneaux. And a pleasure working with you. You're welcome to come back any time." She held out her hand to shake his. "And make sure you lock up when you leave."

He took her hand. Firm shake. He liked that in a woman. It meant confidence, and if there was one thing Joanna Killian was about, it was confidence. "So you just up and leave?"

"Yep. That's what a circuit doctor does. A couple of days here, a couple of days there."

"And when does the circuit doctor have time for a personal life?"

"Never." She stood and headed to the examining room

where she'd put the cot. "Goodnight, Chay. See you when I get back if you're still here. If not, have a safe trip."

Chay sat there alone for several minutes, thinking about happiness. He was happy, he thought. Nice life, nice medical practice. All the advantages. Joanna was happy, too. *Happy here!* And it was all wrapped up in her work. She lived in an impoverished little town, barely had supplies enough to run a clinic, worked ungodly hours. No advantages at all, and she was still happy. "Amazing," he murmured, as he finally slogged up the stairs. "Amazing woman." It didn't seem right, this life she was living. It was too hard for someone to do alone. But that's what she did and she didn't complain. And him… Well, he complained if his golf game every other Saturday morning got rained out. Different worlds was right.

After a quick shower he fell into bed, sure he would fall asleep the instant his head hit the pillow. But he didn't because he couldn't get Joanna out of his mind. The pillows, the sheets smelled like her tonight, he thought as he lowered himself onto the bed. A slight hint of lilac. Maybe her soap, since Joanna seemed the practical type, meaning she'd buy a patient reading glasses rather than treat herself to a luxury like perfume. A woman like Joanna deserved perfume, though. She also deserved her bed, and not some uncomfortable cot stuck in an examining room.

Even so, Chay lingered another few minutes, enjoying the scent of her surrounding him. Breathing it in, fantasizing… Beyond his lowered eyelids Joanna was naked, and this time it had nothing to do with him catching her accidentally. She was pulling off her T-shirt for him, slipping out of her jeans, pulling off that infernal baseball cap she always tucked that glorious red mane up under. And she was coming to his bed…straight into his open arms… He opened his eyes. Except Joanna didn't have time for a social life and, with any luck, in another day or so his own social life would be back in Chicago.

He got out of bed, plodded down the stairs and went straight to the examining room. "I was going to let you have the bed tonight since you're going to be on the road tomorrow. But as I'm going with you, I've decided to keep the bed myself. Just thought you should know that." That said, he plodded back to bed, wondering what in the world he'd just done. And why.

"Sorry I missed spending yesterday afternoon with you," Chay said to his mother after giving her an affectionate peck on the cheek. The diner opened early, and Joanna wasn't even up yet when he'd left. He'd gone first to his grandmother's house to gather a few of his old clothes out of her attic—jeans and T-shirts instead of his usual khakis and polos, plus a pair of comfortable cowboy boots he'd bought twenty years ago. And his hat, of course. Traditional cowboy style, black, with a white feather in it. The feather was supposed to signify that he was an Indian, although he didn't know if it really did, but it looked good. It had been a long time since he'd seen these clothes, and Macawi hadn't said a word when he'd told her why he was taking them. She'd simply kissed him on the cheek and given him that devilish glint.

"Joanna called after you left for Billings. That was a good thing you did, Chayton. I'm glad you were able to help Michael. She said he might have lost his leg otherwise."

He didn't want to talk about it, because that simply brought him closer to a place he didn't want to be. And he couldn't afford close. Not to Rising Sun, not to the people there. "I saw Dad at the Red Elks'," he said, purposely changing the subject. "Did he mention it to you?" Not a chance, Chay knew. Not a damned chance.

Wenona shook her head, confirming what he already knew. "No, but I guessed as much. He wasn't in a very good mood last night when he came home. Refused his supper, and went to bed early."

"He's not looking good, Mom."

"He's tired."

"He needs to see a doctor… Joanna. After she gets back."

"He won't do that."

Wenona tried to scurry away to get the coffeepot, but Chay reached across the counter and grabbed her hand. "I'm going out with Joanna for a couple of days. When we get back I'll go talk to him."

"He won't listen to you, Chayton. You know that."

"Maybe he won't listen in his heart, but he'll hear the words." And perhaps that was the best he could do for his father. "Now, how about you go rustle up some biscuits for me to take on the road?" He kissed the back of her hand. "And a large cola, extra cherry. Make that two. We got to bed late last night and Joanna might need a little sugar and caffeine boost to get herself going this morning."

"*We* got to bed?" Wenona shot him a brooding scowl. "What do you mean, *we*?"

"As in me upstairs, her downstairs. Now, about those biscuits…"

"What are you doing there?" Joanna asked, tossing a duffel bag into the back of her Jeep. Chayton was sitting in the passenger seat, looking a whole lot better than she'd ever seen him look. Jeans, T-shirt, and that hat. Gorgeous was an understatement. He was drop-dead and beyond, if there was anything beyond drop-dead gorgeous. Made to order, if she could have ordered, but she simply didn't have time. Not even for casual. It was a pity. She liked him. Sure, he had issues to deal with, but didn't everybody? He was a good doctor, compassionate even if he didn't want to admit it, and perfect company for a lonely girl in the Big Open. Big pity.

"Waiting for you."

"Waiting for me to do what?"

"Leave."

"And?" She saw his duffel bag in the back. Now she was confused.

"And I'm going with you." He held out the giant-sized soda. "It's not too early for this, is it? I know some people go with coffee or orange juice to start the day, but since I couldn't find a café…"

She took the drink and noticed the basket of hot biscuits sitting between the two seats. "What's this about, Chay?"

"Like I said last night, I'm going with you. When I told you, you didn't object, so…"

"When you told me I must have been asleep, because I don't remember it." That was a bit of a lie, actually. She did remember, but she'd been afraid it had only been a dream. Or wishful thinking. And wishful thinking not so much as a doctor who wanted help, but as a woman who was already getting excited over the prospect of spending a couple of days with him. He wasn't the talkative type, they were complete opposites in just about every sense of the word, and she bet if she searched every inch of the nearly two thousand square miles of Hawk Reservation, she wouldn't find a common goal between them. Apparently, that made it a hormonal reaction to him—her hormones getting all hot and bothered over his. But that would work, for a couple of days. Besides, going from one job to another, she hadn't had a real holiday in years. A couple of days of splashing hormones with Chay might just give her a little of that on-holiday feeling. A feeling she didn't have to act on, of course.

Just a feeling…just a feeling… Say it three times and she

might even believe it. She hoped so. "It's all about work," she told him, a little too adamantly. It almost sounded silly. "You understand that, don't you?"

He tilted his hat up to look at her. "Uh-huh," he drawled lazily. "Work."

"And it's not the kind of medicine to which you're accustomed. We're going to be looking at hemorrhoids and fungal infections. Everyday ailments, and they come in all varieties."

He tilted his hat back down and slid down into the seat. "Uh-huh. Sore butts and athlete's foot."

"You need bedding."

"Got it."

"If it rains, we may have to go into Fishback Creek on horseback."

"I can ride."

"Bareback."

He tilted his hat back up, cocked his head at her and grinned. "My people haven't ridden bareback for a century. But if that's what you want to do, go for it." Then the hat went back down.

"Why are you doing this?" she asked. Naturally, she wanted him to tell her he was looking forward to two days with her, riding with her, working with her, sleeping with… Well, she was going to let that one go for now. But an inkling of a reason having to do with *him* wanting to be with *her* might have been pleasant. Most likely, though, he was working out some kind of deep-rooted guilt. That was the way it always was, it seemed. That was why Paul, her ex, had taken up her dream long enough to slip the wedding ring on her finger. He had been suffering some kind of misplaced societal guilt over the conditions of the poor at the time. But when he'd got into those conditions with her down in Haiti, and had discovered even his guilt wasn't enough to compel him to do the hard, dirty work required, he had quit practice to write a textbook on the very thing he couldn't, or wouldn't, do himself. Then he went on the lecture circuit around the world, talking about the medical needs of the underclass, and had made quite a success of it. But while he had been out talking, she had been back in Haiti, doing. Two worlds, so far apart they never had got back together.

Once bitten, twice shy. She simply wasn't going to allow Chay, in his different world, to bite. Not hard anyway.

But maybe just a nibble?

"Why am I doing this?" he muttered from under his hat. "I saw you naked. Remember? Gorgeous, perfect, a sight to remember. And I was hoping that out there in the wilds, I might just get lucky."

Joanna forced back a laugh. A little nibble might not be so bad after all. "Well, Mr Lucky, how about you scoot over and drive while I sit back, relax, drink soda and eat biscuits?" Not bad at all.

About ten miles outside of Rising Sun, Joanna hit Chay with the one thing she knew wasn't going to make him happy. "I've got to stop at the ranch and give some immunizations to the workers there." She watched him for a reaction, but he didn't even flinch. "Did you hear me?"

"I heard you."

"And?"

"And nothing. We stop at the ranch."

"What about your dad?"

"He'll stay away from me. I can deal with it."

"I'm sorry about the way he treated you yesterday."

"He didn't *treat* me any way." Chay swerved off the road to the drive leading up to the main gates of Hawk Cattle Ranch.

Actually, calling it a cattle ranch was a bit of a misnomer. Over the years the operation had added a dairy concern to provide fresh milk to the reservation, chickens for the eggs, sheep for the wool, and a farm rich with barley and several root crops, including potatoes and sugar beets. It employed hundreds of people throughout the entire reservation, and Chay's dad was in charge. He'd gone to the community college in Fort Peck, had earned his degrees in agriculture and business management, then returned home as was expected of him. As had been expected of Chay. There were no secrets on the reservation, and Joanna was uneasy with this first stop. But she had the flu vaccine ready to go, and it was her job. "Look, you can leave me here, go back to Rising Sun then come back in a couple of hours. Or stay in the Jeep and take a nap or something. There's really no need for you to—"

"Like I told you, he'll avoid me, Joanna. And I can deal with that. OK? It's not a big deal."

"OK." She may have said the word, but nothing about this felt OK to her. And Chay certainly didn't sound OK. Unfortunately, there was nothing she could do. This appointment had been arranged for weeks, and she had to follow through. But she did feel badly for him. She also felt badly for Leonard. Being estranged from someone you should love, and who, deep down, you probably still did, had to be tough. "Look, I'm going to set up in the administration building. I have a list of the men and women who will be getting shots, and all we do is check them off when we give them. They'll be waiting."

And they were. More than two hundred people, if everyone on her list showed up. The line wound down the hall into the makeshift clinic that had been set up for her, then outside and all the way around the building. Her accommodation was simply a table and a chair in an otherwise empty storage closet, and one by one each of those two hundred people would wander in, roll up a shirt sleeve for the vaccination, then wander back out. "Maybe we could double the line,'' she said, ''since you're here. You take one line, I take the other.''

Within seconds Chay was outside, organizing the lines, giving instructions, apparently in his native language because she didn't understand a word. But the people there must have, because they split into two lines and shortly the flu inoculations were underway. The process took less than two hours, and as Joanna and Chay were cleaning up the room afterward, sealing all the disposable syringes into the proper red container, Chay picked up the list. ''My father's name isn't checked off,'' he commented, his voice as dry as the hard, cracked, dry ground outside.

''I was going to stop by his office on the way out, see if he still wants his vaccination.'' She'd seen Leonard in the line when they'd arrived, and had watched him leave the line when Chay stepped out of the Jeep.

''I'll do it.''

''Are you sure? He might refuse you.''

''He probably will.'' No more words. Chay picked up the medicine vial, alcohol swabs and a syringe and headed down the hall.

From the doorway, Joanna watched him approach his father's office, watched him reach out to take hold of the doorknob. He hesitated for a moment before he opened the door and entered, and her heart ached a little for him. *She'd* lived through the ultimate separation from her parents in their deaths, but to be so greatly separated when that parent was only a few feet away? She'd lived through that, too. So, yes, her heart did ache a little.

''I'm here to see Leonard Ducheneaux,'' Chay said to the secretary. He didn't recognize her. The last time he'd been into this office Rose Yellow Cloud had been his father's secretary, and she'd retired and moved to Florida more than a dozen years ago.

''Do you have an appointment?'' the secretary asked. The nameplate on her desk read MARILYN DUBONET. He didn't recognize her, didn't recognize her name, except that he'd gone to school with Gary Gray Hawk Dubonet. His wife perhaps? Chay thought about asking, but didn't. Gary had ridiculed him for leaving Hawk.

''No. I'm the doctor.'' He held up the vial and syringe. ''Mr Ducheneaux was on the list for a vaccination, but he didn't show up. This will take only a minute.''

''Sure. Go on in. Leonard's going over the books right now, and I think he'd probably welcome the break, even if it is a shot.'' She lowered her voice. ''He needs new glasses, I think. Lots of headaches lately. And eye strain. But he's too stubborn to get checked. So, as you're a doctor, maybe you could suggest something while you're in there.''

His dad was too stubborn? Sounded familiar. ''Thanks,'' he said, finding suddenly that his feet felt like lead weights. He was faced with a simple task really. Go in, get rejected, leave. Ten seconds tops. Twelve if he mentioned getting his eyes checked. But Chay's feet didn't want to move. ''Um, did you get your vaccination?'' he asked Marilyn. *Stalling for time, you big coward?*

''Sure did, from DocJo.''

He nodded, not so much listening to her as trying to find another way to stall.

''You can go in now,'' she said again.

''Thanks.''

''And I think Leonard has a check for DocJo. He subsidized the shots for the ranch this year.''

Chayton nodded as he walked toward the door. It was simple pine, a flat panel, nothing immense or oppressive. So why did it feel so immense and oppressive to him? ''Thank you,'' he said as he twisted the brass knob.

Pushing the door open, Chayton saw his father sitting at the desk straight ahead. Same desk that had always been there. Same shelves behind it, same blinds at the window. Apart from the computer on the desk, nothing had changed. Except his father. "I've come to give you your flu vaccination."

Leonard looked up at Chay, but there was no sign of recognition on his face. And as before, at the Red Elks', he said nothing.

"I didn't find your name crossed off on the list."

Leonard's reply was to stand and roll up the sleeve of his blue and white striped cotton shirt. Once his upper arm was revealed sufficiently, he stepped away from his desk and turned his arm toward Chay. But there was no greeting, not even a glance in his direction. No emotion whatsoever from the man who used to bring him to this office and let him play boss.

"You're going to feel a little prick," Chay said just before he administered the shot. Funny, he remembered his father's arms being larger, more muscular. They were slight now. Not too thin, but too slight for a man who should have been robust, even at his age. "There, that's it." He placed the obligatory bandage over the shot site even though his father didn't bleed. Then he watched his father roll down his sleeve and return to his chair behind the desk. Once there, Leonard pushed a check across the desk to Chay without uttering a word, then swivelled to the computer screen, put on his glasses, and returned to work.

"Macawi's worried about you," Chay said after he pocketed the check made out to the Rising Sun Medical Clinic. He didn't expect a response, so he wasn't disappointed when he didn't get one. "She thinks you're not feeling well and she'd like you to see a doctor. And your secretary is concerned about your headaches."

No response.

"Have you been ill lately? Experienced any unusual symptoms?"

No response again, but, of course, Chay didn't expect one.

"Maybe you should schedule an appointment with Joanna. Just a routine physical to make sure everything's OK."

Nothing. Not even a passing glance to acknowledge Chay's presence there.

"Look, I know it's none of my business. But Macawi's worried about you and, if for no other reason than to make her feel better, you need to get yourself checked by someone. You don't look good—" He'd almost called him *Dad*, but had stopped short of it. "My mother and Macawi both depend on you, and you have an obligation to them to take care of yourself. Plus there's your obligation to the ranch and the people who work and live here. I'm going with Joanna for a couple of days to some of the outlying areas, then I'll be back. If you'd like me to check you then, I'd be glad to. If you'd prefer Joanna do it, that's fine, too. Or even make an appointment up at Fort Peck. Whatever suits you, as long as you do it." This time he didn't wait for a response. He simply turned and walked out of the office and straight into Joanna, who was waiting in the hallway for him.

"Want me to try and give it to him?" she asked. "The shot? He might be more receptive to me."

"He took the shot."

"And?"

"And he gave me a check for services."

"That's it? You two didn't…"

"No. We didn't. And we won't." He'd been fine with that for eighteen years. But now, seeing his father looking the way he did, he wasn't sure any more. Unfortunately, his father *was* still sure, and everything Chay had said in there had fallen on deaf ears.

CHAPTER SIX

INITIALLY, somewhere in the first twenty-five miles on the road to Fishback Creek, Joanna had thought about attempting a little conversation with Chay, but there was absolutely nothing about him that suggested he would respond to her in any way. His body language said it all—rigid, unyielding, belligerent. And that scowl on his face… If ever there was a black cloud on the horizon, Chay's scowl was it. He was a savage summer storm ready to rip open into a torrential downpour, and she didn't want to be the one to start the ugly deluge. So she kept quiet as he drove. And she kept her eyes focused squarely on the flat, grassy badlands off to the side of the road. It was a great big vast emptiness out there—mile after relentless mile of boring scenery, but infinitely safer than the scenery sitting right next to her.

He was a man possessed, she thought. Or tormented. Of course she knew why. Another blow from his father. Sure, he'd been expecting it, but she suspected that deep down Chay had been hoping for a different outcome. Otherwise he wouldn't have been the one to go into Leonard's office in the first place. It was a little hope springing eternal before being dashed to pieces. So she was allowing Chay his solitude right now, even though she was wedged in pretty close to him. Close enough to catch a trace of aftershave every now and then. Something with lime. Her favorite flavor. And he was so nice in lime.

After an hour, Chay still hadn't said a word. They'd been setting a bat-out-of-hell pace for so long her legs were beginning to ache from all the bumps they were hitting. It was like Chay was aiming for them, trying to do some kind of

71

cathartic maneuver in the form of pothole therapy. And she was feeling every last pothole in her bladder. "Can you stop? Comfort break," she finally said.

He didn't respond.

"I said, stop, I've got to…"

He slammed on the brakes so hard that, seat belt or not, Joanna lurched forward. "One more time like that and I won't have to go any more," she grumbled, climbing out.

"So go," he snapped.

Go. That was easy for him to say. Not so easy for her to do, though, considering that everything she could see was wide open and without a speck of privacy. Not a tree, not a rock, not a little valley or even a ditch. Absolutely no privacy to be had, except maybe that little scrub bush sitting about a hundred yards off the road. Not much, but a little seclusion was better than none at all.

"Where the hell are you going?" he yelled when she was about halfway to the bush.

"Somewhere you won't see me," she yelled back.

"I've already seen you. Remember?"

Yep, she remembered.

Doubling her speed to the bush, she was almost there when Chay started sounding the horn at her. Long, impatient blasts, one after another. She'd tried to respect his mood for the last hour, she'd endured his terrible driving, but this was too much.

By the time Joanna was back at the Jeep, she had a good case of anger blistering at her. "Get out," she snapped. "I'm driving."

His hat was tipped over his face now, his arms folded across his chest, and he didn't budge.

"Did you hear me? I said *I'm* driving. It's my car, so scoot over and ride, or get out and walk."

"I'm sorry," he muttered from under his hat.

"For what?"

"For everything up until now. You know, blanket apology for all my offenses."

"For being a jerk."

"Sure. That's included."

"And you're not just saying that so you won't have to walk?"

He tilted his hat up to look at her. "I'm saying it because I mean it. You don't deserve the way I've been acting." A lazy grin crossed his mouth. "When a girl needs some privacy, she shouldn't be subjected to roadside harassment. So I'm sorry. Really."

Damn, he was hard to stay angry at. That smile captured her, those eyes held her, and she believed he meant what he'd said. For all his moods, Chay Ducheneaux was sincere. "Apology accepted, but that doesn't change the fact that I still want to drive."

"My mother never learned. My father wouldn't allow it. He always said he would take her wherever she needed to go and I guess she never felt the need for independence of any sort. Damned shame."

"Independence comes in a lot of forms, Chay. Maybe your mother simply never wanted to drive, and it has nothing to do with her independence, and everything to do with her choice."

"Some choices are hard," he said.

"And some are easy. Just depends on what you want, I suppose. And I want to drive."

Chay grinned at her. "Are you a good driver, Joanna?"

"Better than you are. I actually try avoiding the holes."

"Far be it for me to stand in the way of the lady's choice." Scooting over into the passenger's seat, Chay slumped down and pulled his hat back over his eyes. "By the way, those are great binoculars you've got. I found them under the seat. Amazing what they can pick up at a distance. Great zoom capacity. Nice detail when you want to look at something like a scrub bush a hundred yards away. Real nice detail.''

In spite of herself, Joanna laughed, knowing he was teasing. ''I suppose if you're that desperate for a peek, you're welcome.''

''Not desperate. Just trying to stir up some fond memories.''

''Isn't that the way with guys? They see you naked just one time and they get all silly and sentimental over it.''

''Apparently you haven't seen the side of you that I have because it's definitely worth silly and sentimental.''

''And that's a compliment?''

''Of the highest order. Believe me. It's not one that I've paid very often.''

''Have you ever been married, Chay?'' she asked. Not that it mattered. But she was curious.

''Hell, no!''

''Spoken like a man with true conviction.'' Not that it mattered again, but she felt a little disappointment sweep through her. It was silly to think she could have any feelings for him other than casual, but there was no denying the fact that she'd felt a little jab in her belly over his quick, almost cutting response. Rebound. That was what had caused it. The ink on her divorce papers was barely dry, and Chay was the first man in her life, in any capacity, since then. And such a gorgeous one at that. Definitely rebound.

Still, a fond little sigh for something that would never be touched her lips.

''Actually, spoken like a man with a true aversion,'' he said.

True aversion? ''Are you gay?'' That thought had never crossed her mind before. ''Do you prefer men, and your fascination with my butt is your cover-up?''

He chuckled. ''Believe me. I prefer women. I just don't have a burning need for permanence.''

"Well, I can't fault you there because I sure didn't have a need for permanence in my first marriage. I was ready to get out after a couple of months." And she had. In and out in less than a year.

"Did he fight to keep you?"

"Nope. He was as happy to get out as I was."

"Then he apparently didn't have a proper appreciation for the finer things in life."

"Meaning my butt?"

Chay tipped his hat back up again and looked over at her, and for a moment what she saw in his eyes was profoundly serious. "Meaning his loss, Joanna. And he'll probably never know how much he's lost." Then he lightened up and winked. "And your butt, too."

He pulled his hat back down over his eyes at the same time goose-bumps rose on her arms. That look in his eyes…the serious one. She wanted to buy into that sincerity. She truly did, but she wouldn't allow it. Still, brushing her hand over the chill bumps frolicking up and down her arm, she was more acutely aware of him sitting next to her than ever before. *His loss, Joanna. And he'll probably never know how much.*

A completely new outbreak of bumps rose on her arms as she remembered the words.

Finally, after a very tense hour and a half, they rolled into Fishback Creek. Normally it took a good two hours to get there from the ranch, so Chay's personal thundercloud, translating to a heavy foot on the gas pedal, had worked to their advantage, because Joanna hated that part of the job—the interminable hours of driving through nowhere. Granted, Fishback Creek was barely a notch above nowhere. Just a couple hundred people, mostly women and children as the men worked at the ranch and stayed there in the bunkhouse during the week. But it was civilization all the same, and after all that time on the road with Chay she was glad for the relief of the friendly faces she knew she'd be greeting within the next few minutes.

"We have that little building down there at the end of town." Fishback Creek consisted of one short street with four buildings including the school, a gas station-grocery store combination, a deserted mechanic's garage, which was where Joanna set up, and the town building which served to hold meetings, church services, and assorted social functions. There was also a dotting of woodframe houses along the street. Neat, plain, small. "We're giving immunizations here today, and I have a few follow-up appointments. I'll also see anyone who thinks they need to be seen and a couple of people I think need to be seen."

"My God, this is awful," he muttered. "I don't remember it being so small."

"Population's on the decline. Declining throughout all the towns on the reservation, actually. Nothing here to keep them, I suppose." Nothing but their heritage, but that wasn't enough to hold them to their land any more. These people wanted more, needed more. And she couldn't blame them for going after it. "Did you know that Duchesne is completely gone now? Ghost town. No one lives there any more." The last of its residents had packed up and moved out about the time she'd come to Hawk. "And Claremont is about to do the same. There are only about a hundred people left there, although some of the old-timers are holding tough, trying to stay."

"And my father snubs me for leaving all this." He laughed bitterly. "I really can't blame them. There's no reason to stay."

"Except heritage and tradition," Joanna said. "Pride in who they are, where they come from."

"So are you like everybody else around here who thinks I'm some kind of bad person for leaving?"

"I think you're a good doctor, Chay. A great doctor, after what I saw you do for Michael. The rest is for you to decide. We're going to be spending the night here, by the way."

He looked around, frowning. "Where?"

"In the garage where I set up clinic. It's clean, it makes a good little medical office, and normally when I'm here someone takes pity and fixes me a nice meal or two."

"I'm betting there's not a bed associated with this God-forsaken overnighter, is there?" He grinned. "Or a Jacuzzi. After that ride, I could go for a nice Jacuzzi right about now."

His mood was lightening. She was glad, because the people here were nice and they didn't deserve his bad mood. "Guess that all depends on your definition of bed. But the good news is, we do have indoor plumbing, electricity and running water." No way she would tell him it was cold running water.

"So where do we start?"

"With lunch. I'm starving." Joanna waved at Phyllis Whirlwind who was scurrying in their direction with a wicker hamper full of goodies. Cakes, cookies, the best deep-fried pies Joanna had ever eaten. Actually, they were the only deep-fried pies she'd ever eaten, and after her first, a yummy black raspberry, she'd become a true addict. So many good things to eat, and Phyllis was a marvelous cook. She was also diabetic, as was her thirteen-year-old daughter, Collette. The condition wasn't a good combination for Phyllis's cooking and eating habits, but so far neither Phyllis nor Collette had taken their disease seriously.

"I have a nice salad for you today, DocJo," Phyllis announced proudly. "From my garden. Nice fresh greens."

Promising, Joanna thought.

"And enough for him, too."

"This is Dr Chayton Ducheneaux," Joanna said.

"Chay?" Phyllis's eyes lit up. "I've heard so much about you."

Chay took the hamper from Phyllis. "And how's Jack? We were friends when we were kids...did a lot of fishing together. And we roomed together up at the community college at Fort Peck." He chuckled. "Got ourselves into trouble a few times. Can't wait to catch up with him, see if he can still put back the beer like he used to."

Joanna sucked in a deep breath and held it. Chay couldn't have known. "He died last month, Chay," she said, sparing Phyllis the grief of talking about it. It was still so fresh, so painful to talk about, even for Joanna. God only knew how it was for Phyllis. "Kidney failure."

"I...I didn't..." Chay stopped, swallowed hard, drew in a deep, steadying breath. "I'm so sorry," he said, his voice so quiet and somber Joanna had to strain to hear him. "He was a good man. Smart. A good friend. I'm...I'm so sorry."

"Thank you, Chay," Phyllis managed, fighting back her tears. "And yes, he could still put back the beer like he did when he was in college." A single tear finally slid down her left cheek. "We miss him, but DocJo did everything she could to help." She smiled at Joanna. "I have to get back to the little ones. But I'll be back for my appointment later on." In leaving she didn't scurry, as she had in coming. Instead, she trudged away slowly, her shoulders slumped, her steps labored. She looked like the grief-stricken woman she was.

"What the hell happened to him?" Chay hissed. "Kidney failure? He was my age, for God's sake."

"Diabetes. Brittle. I couldn't keep ahead of it." Her words sounded a bit dispassionate, she knew, but they weren't. In her six months on Hawk she'd lost six people to diabetes. One death for each of her months there. And there was nothing dispassionate about every bad test result she saw, every complication she tried to treat, every new diagnosis she made, every patient she lost. Nothing dispassionate at all. "Phyllis is diabetic, too. So's her oldest daughter. The results of their latest A1C tests are horrible." A1C referred to a test to determine an average blood-sugar level for the previous two to three months. It was used as a diagnostic tool to keep track of a diabetic's overall condition. "Norm is six or below from someone who isn't diabetic, seven for someone who is and who's responding to treatment. Collette is at eight right now. Way, way too high for a child, and she needs treatment. Phyllis is at ten, which means she's in danger. And she's bringing us a basket full of cookies."

Chay whistled. "And I'm assuming they don't take any kind of medication."

"Most of the people around here won't take insulin shots, but I do leave pills for them. I leave pills all over the reservation, Chay. Some people do a good job managing their condition, but a lot don't. Jack Whirlwind was in end-stage renal failure—a complication of his diabetes—when I got here. He was going to Billings several times a week for dialysis, while Phyllis stayed at home baking, and eating, cookies. And letting her kids eat like she does."

"So they accept the risk. There's nothing you can do to force them to modify their habits."

"You're right. I can't force them. But maintaining such a potentially devastating disease out here where there's no support, where it's simply easier to revert back to the old ways, is damned hard. I really think they mean to take care of themselves, at least when I'm here. But I'm not here all the time."

"And diabetes is really that widespread on the reservation?"

"That widespread," she said glumly. "I have three new diagnoses here alone."

* * *

Lunch was hasty. A nice salad, actually. The two of them opted to split a fried pie, and skip over the rest of the sweets. As they were eating, Chay couldn't get his mind off of Jack Whirlwind. Or off Jack's wife and daughter, for that matter. Sure, he'd read the statistics and the journal articles about the alarming increase of diabetes in American Indians. But he sure as hell had never expected to come face to face with it on such a personal level. And now he was left to wonder about his father. Some of the symptoms fit. At least the ones he'd seen did—weight loss, tiredness, eyesight problems, headaches.

"How do you do it?" he finally asked Joanna.

"One patient at a time. That's the only way you *can* do it or it will drive you insane."

He watched her setting out the supplies for the immunizations. It was a mundane task, and one she was approaching with such optimism. He admired her for that. Admired her for what he saw, admired her for what he didn't see. She was the kind of doctor he should have been, the kind he'd never found the heart to be.

"Why don't you let me handle the shots this afternoon? I can do that while you see patients. That way, maybe we can get done early enough to go for a walk later on. There was this place down by the creek my dad used to bring me when he was up here on ranch business." A nice place, greener than most places in the Big Open. Joanna would like it, he thought. Maybe they could take a few of Phyllis Whirlwind's treats and have a picnic.

Joanna smiled. "I haven't had a real evening off in…well, weeks, probably. It's been so long I can't remember."

"Then it's a date."

"A date," she agreed.

A date with Joanna. That, if nothing else, made staying at Hawk an extra few days worthwhile.

*   *   *

Between immunizations and patients, the afternoon breezed by quicker than she'd expected it to. Normally these trips dragged out well into the night, but by suppertime her day was done. Completely done, and she was looking forward to her *date*.

Angel Dupuis had drawn the supper chore, and thankfully it had turned out to be some hearty vegetable soup with fresh bread. Perfect, as Joanna had stopped by the Whirlwinds' to deliver a month's supply of medicine to Phyllis and Collette and had witnessed their evening fare— macaroni and cheese, mashed potatoes, bread and heaps of fried pies. She hadn't lectured them about it. She didn't do that. It would alienate them, and that would be the worst thing that could happen. So she'd handed over the pills, given them instruction on how to take them for the hundredth time in six months, left a pamphlet about diabetic eating habits, refused a generous, heaping plateful of their meal and had hurried away.

"So how far is this place?" she asked, as she and Chay hiked south on an overgrown trail leading out of town. The prairie grasses came up to her knees and looked like they hadn't been beaten down since for ever.

"About a mile. We could have taken the Jeep, but I like to walk. Especially at night, when it's quiet." He chuckled. "In Chicago you never get quiet. The best you can do is shut your window and hope most of the noise stays outside."

"You like that?" His stride was much longer than hers, and even at an easy pace she was finding it difficult to keep up with him. "The noise? I used to live in Baltimore and I hated all the noise."

"You get used to it."

"I never did. Could you slow down a little bit?"

"I could carry you."

She knew he was joking, but hearing him say it caused

shivers to shoot up and down her arms. "I snuck a few extra bites of a fried pie before we started. After that, I don't think you could lift me."

"I work out."

"I noticed." Noticed in a big way! In fact, every time he wasn't looking, she was noticing. Not smart but, oh, so good for her poor, tired eyes. Nothing better than a fabulous body like Chay's to pop them right back open when they were fighting so hard to sleep.

"I noticed you noticing a couple of times." He reached out and took her hand. "So I guess that makes it worth all the money I spend at the health club to keep myself in shape. At least, I hope it does."

"You fishing for a compliment, Doctor?"

"Don't need one, after the way I've seen you checking me out."

This was the first time they'd been away from medicine, and his father, and the affairs of the reservation, and especially away from their differences, and even though they were walking hand in hand through the middle of heaven only knew where, it did feel like a real date to her. All the anticipation and tingling over a first date with someone. All the expectations of a night out with someone. She...well, she wasn't sure how she felt about. There was a complex mixture of emotions going on, both his and hers, and she didn't want to ruin the moment trying to unravel them into something she could define better. So for now she was going to think about it as being out with someone who more than attracted her in the physical sense, someone she absolutely did like, and that was as far as she would allow it to go. For now.

"This is lovely," she said once they'd settled into a plush, grassy spot on top of a small butte overlooking the creek. Sitting atop a blanket Chay had brought along, they were nestled into a few scrub trees, nothing really secluded, yet very intimate, just the two of them together under all that fading sky above. The red sunset in the distance warmed the surroundings and Joanna had the feeling that no one had been there before—nothing or no one but the elk she saw silhouetted in the distance beyond the creek, and the lonely coyote who was hidden somewhere in the evening shadows howling for his lady love, or warning her about the human intruders in his territory. Or maybe he was howling at nothing at all, howling because he felt like it. She liked that—howling because he felt like it. She'd come out here with Chay because she felt like it. No other reason. She and the coyote, with similar motives.

Drawing in a deep breath of pure, fresh air, Joanna finally relaxed. This was indeed a place for a long look at unobstructed beauty, and for the first few minutes there Joanna did nothing but drink it all in. "It's amazing," she whispered as reverently as she would have in a great cathedral. In a way, this *was* a great cathedral, one with perfect architecture that far surpassed anything sculpted. "During the day everything seems so…"

"Desolate," Chay supplied.

Joanna nodded. "Desolate. But look at it now. At night. I've never seen it this way." Before tonight she'd had neither the time nor the inclination to look. And describing it now as breathtaking didn't come close to painting the true picture of it…of this wilderness all around them. Nothing did. "Did Leonard bring you here often?"

"Not often, which meant that when I did get to come it was special." Chay tossed his hat aside and propped himself against a small rock outcropping. "When I was a kid I really wanted trees in my yard. Trees anywhere. Something to climb, something to hang a swing from. But out here we don't get trees, not real ones anyway, and I don't think I appreciated the sunrises and sunsets, and especially the unbelievable skyscapes until my dad started bringing me here to the creek. And when you see all this, you realize that the only thing a tree would do is clutter the view.''

"Do you miss it?'' she asked, settling in next to him. "Living in Chicago, you have trees and water, but all this…do you miss it?''

"Don't think I knew how much until just now. And the best part is, in another few minutes, when the sun goes down, you're going to see the blackest skies and whitest stars you've ever seen in your life. Millions of stars just hanging up there. In the city you don't see stars, not like here. I used to love to make a wish on the first star I saw at night.''

"Star light, star bright, first star I see tonight,'' Joanna recited wistfully. She'd done the same thing, too. "What did you wish for?''

"Trees.'' He chuckled. "Lots of trees, and I guess that wish came true because I've got them where I live.''

She'd wished for a family. Of course, that had never come true. *Star light, star bright…* Joanna sighed, contented to let him sweep her along on his nostalgic ride. This was a wonderful place for a first date. Wonderful and romantic. She was just beginning to settle into the whole sensual ambiance of the evening, anticipating what might come next— maybe a kiss, maybe more—when Chay suddenly jumped up and headed down the side of the butte to the creek. "Going wading,'' he called back. "Want to come?''

Their first date…wading! Not what she'd expected. Definitely not what she'd have written in her personal journal, if she'd kept one. *My first date with Chay—we waded.* Not at all what she was hoping for. "Sure,'' she called back, somewhat surprised, somewhat disappointed, somewhat relieved. "Why not?'' Kicking off her shoes and going barefoot in the creek would have about the same effect as a cold shower, which was probably for the best since she'd been getting caught up in the romanticism of the moment, and even beginning to hope about all the places that moment would lead to. She knew it would lead Chay right back to Chicago, and that was as far as she should have gone with it. Problem was, even knowing the end of the story wasn't stopping the thoughts from creeping in.

Joanna sat on the butte for a minute, watching him play in the creek. It had taken her months to develop any kind of feelings for Paul. Months and months, and even then she hadn't been sure about them. It was more like she'd forced them into place, then accepted them for what they'd been.

But with Chay the feelings came easily. *Too easily.*

That was bad. Even though the consequences were all so clear to her, she was willing to accept them, regardless. And she was beginning to understand how desperately *regardless* was going to hurt.

CHAPTER SEVEN

"No!" SHE squealed, slipping over the slick shale on the creek bottom to get away from him. "Don't you dare pull me down."

"You can't run fast enough to get away from me." Chay laughed as he reached out to grab Joanna by the back of her T-shirt. "And I have some experience playing in a creek, so give up, Joanna. You're going down, and you can do it the easy way or the hard way."

"Wanna bet?" She squirmed free of him, then, in water up to her knees, she jumped into the night shadows of a scraggly bush overhanging the creek and held her breath until Chayton passed by her. "Oh, Chay," she called from her hiding place. "I'm waiting."

She could hear him splashing closer and closer, and she held her breath and waited until she could sense his presence so close to her that she could reach out and touch him, even though the bush blocked her view. Then she lunged out of the shadows and knocked him over, laughing as he lost his balance and went all the way down. "Serves you right," she said, bending down and splashing water at him, "thinking you're better at this than I am. I'll have you know that West Virginia has lots of creeks and I've had my feet in a fair share of them."

"You're so bad," Chay said, struggling to his feet. "And you're about to get all wet."

"And you're *so* back in the water." As he pushed himself up to his knees she tried to shove him over again, but he caught her by the arm and pulled her down in with him. "You're going to pay for that, Chayton Ducheneaux," she squealed as she struggled to find her footing. But he kept pulling her back to him. "Once you let me up…"

"Big talk, that's all you are. Big talk." He laughed. "And all wet, just like I said."

It had been years since she'd been wading or, as it was turning out, swimming. Last time she'd been immersed in water other than that intended for a bath or shower, it had been a swollen, muddy creek in Haiti and she'd been wading across it to get to a village on the other side. TB outbreak, and she'd been the only doctor for hundreds of miles.

"Big talk?" She was glad it was dark, otherwise Chay would have been getting his very own wet T-shirt show right about now. She'd opted for braless tonight, somewhat for the heat, mostly for the comfort. And, OK, maybe she'd been jumping a bit ahead with Chay. There was some chemistry going on, they were two consenting adults, he had no expectations and neither did she. Not really. "You think I'm just big talk? Well, you think wrong, Doctor. I never talk if I can't deliver."

Twisting out of his clutch, Joanna turned and splashed him, then tried to get back to the relative safety of the bush, but he was too quick for her as he grabbed her by the ankle and dragged her back down into the water before she could fend him off. When she surfaced again, it was straight into his arms. "Like I said, big talk, Joanna, and apparently no delivery. You said you were going to make me pay and I'm still waiting."

"And just what are you willing to pay?" she asked, her face so dangerously close to his that her words came out more as a suggestion than the challenge she'd intended.

"First you've got to tell me what you want from me," he growled.

What she wanted, and couldn't have. Joanna could feel her heart speed up. Crushed to his chest, surely he could feel it, too. "Do you know what this is about?" she whispered, her voice so hoarse with need she barely recognized it as her own.

He reached down to the bottom of her wet shirt and pulled it slowly above her waist, his hand skimming along her flesh causing her to shiver. Upward, ever so slowly, he stopped just before the shirt crossed over her breasts and ran his thumb over her erect nipples, which were more prominent under the soaked fabric than they would have been totally bare. "This is where I stop, Joanna, or go on, depending on what you want. It's tonight for us. Maybe tomorrow or the day after, but…"

She knew the rest, and it didn't matter. She wanted tonight more than anything she could remember wanting in her life. And if that was all there was, so be it. Raising her index finger to Chay's lips, Joanna sucked in a quivering breath. "It is what it is, Chay. I understand that. So this is where you stop talking and start paying." She took hold of his hand and guided it under her wet shirt to her breast. "And if it *is* only tonight, make tonight count."

Chay's fingers lingered there for a few moments, brushing lightly over her nipples. Then he raised her shirt and sought her right breast with his mouth, sucking, nibbling, tweaking her nipple, but only as a foretaste of more to come. For just as she was relaxing to the feel of him there, he moved over to her left breast. Only for a moment again, then he pulled her shirt back down, ran his thumbs over the wet fabric one more time and backed away from her. At several paces, he stopped, merely to stare, as if trying to figure out what he wanted to do.

In the silhouettes made by the moonlight, with only the contours of his body visible to her, he was so gorgeous. Dark, mysterious, brooding. Just watching him watch her made Joanna shiver, made her want to be everything he needed. Chay was a man of subtleties and surprises, and so many conflicts she couldn't anticipate him now. So she merely stood there, watching him watch, and hoping.

After several quiet moments, Joanna's heart began to flutter. Had she been reading the signs incorrectly? Or had he changed his mind about this, and he was looking for a way to back out? If not for the fact that she was unable to move under his stare, she would have backed away, too. Backed away, climbed up to the creek bank and gone back to town. But she couldn't stir herself—shackled there by her own heightening needs and anticipations, she was weighted to the creek bed, praying.

After nearly two minutes of hushed separation between them, embarrassment started to creep over her, so she crossed her arms protectively over her chest. She didn't know what to say, didn't know what to do now, especially when he drew in a sharp breath, then ducked away into the bushes off to the side of the creek.

"OK, am I supposed to come find you?" she finally called to him, not sure if she should. Or if he'd even call back.

"Do you want to come find me?"

She took several tentative steps in the direction of his voice, noticing the water was getting deeper. Another couple of steps and she was wading most of the way up to her hips. "Is it worth my while, Chay?"

"Guess that all depends on what your while is worth, doesn't it?"

Suddenly, a muted splash from behind a bush about five feet away from her caused Joanna to suck in her breath and hold it in nervous expectation. She could back out now. Maybe she should. That would certainly be the unencumbered way through this moment. Probably even the best way. She chuckled. Good thing she didn't always listen to the sensible side of her. "If you want me, Doctor, you'll have to come and get me. Having it my way, right here, is going to be worth *your* while, if you care to come out of the bushes and find out just how much.''

As she said those words, a cloud slipped over the moon, obscuring the little bit of light that had been shining down on them, and Joanna strained to watch for him, to listen for him. But nothing. Not a sound, not even the stirring of a leaf along the creek bank in the gentle summer breeze. ''Chay?'' She finally gave in and called.

''Make it worth my while,'' he growled, stepping up behind her and grabbing her around the waist.

''I didn't hear…'' she gasped, spinning around into his arms.

''Because I didn't want you to hear me. My people are good at that. Being stealthy at the right times.'' He ran his thumb over her lips, then moved to place a brief kiss there. ''Comes in handy,'' he whispered. ''When it counts.''

''Which is when?''

''Right now.'' Pressing himself to her, Chay's hand skimmed underneath the clingy fabric of her T-shirt. ''Nice,'' he said, tracing the line of her ribs to her waist, then over to her belly button. ''I like an inny. So many more possibilities with an inny than an outy.'' His finger lingered there for a moment, to explore the exquisite circle, then moved upward, slowly over her belly. Almost to her breasts, he took a sudden detour back to the waist of her jeans, unzipped them and slowly pulled them down over the curve of her hips. ''Are you wearing those skimpies again like I saw you in the other night?'' His hand went to her hip to pull them along with the jeans, then he moaned. ''Nothing at all? Bad girl.''

''Since you've already seen me in them, I decided to skip the formalities.'' So bold for her. This was nothing like with Paul, in the dark, under the covers, by the book. This was the fantasy she'd read about, and dreamed about and had never thought she would have.

"Very bad girl."

His words made her shiver. His touch, his smell, everything about Chayton Ducheneaux made her shiver, and she was on the verge of wanting him so badly she would have pulled him straight into the water without letting him up until she had everything. But this might be a one and only for them, and that little sentimental spot deep down inside wanted to make it linger. So she pulled back from him. "And you don't like bad girls?" she asked, splashing him playfully.

He took hold of her hand and pressed it to the front of his jeans. "Does that answer your question?" Suddenly, he ducked into the water to press a line of kisses on Joanna's belly, then from her left hip to her right. Removing her jeans all the way, he tossed them to the creek bank when he rose back up. "You won't be needing those for a while."

"Yes, that answers my question," she murmured. Pressing herself to him, she found his zipper and pulled it down. But only until his jeans were riding low on his hips. Then she ran her hand just inside the waistband, brushing her fingers lightly over his erection. He gasped, trying to stifle a moan, and ground himself harder against her hand. But as he'd done with her, she gave him only a moment, then she slid her hand back up to his belly and onward to his chest. Stopping briefly, she pulled off her T-shirt, not as slowly and seductively as she would have liked had he been able to watch in better lighting, but quickly, almost frantically, then tossed it over into a heap with her jeans. "You've got a beautiful chest," she said, pressing her breasts to him. "And does this answer any questions *you* might have?" she added, enjoying the feel of his bare chest on hers. Bare, wet…it was driving her to the brink, when she wasn't ready to go.

"What do you like, Joanna?" he growled, reaching around to her bottom and pulling her hard into him. "Tell me everything.'' Sliding his body down the length of hers until he was nearly submerged, he kissed his way from just below her belly button all the way up to the hollow of her throat. ''Is this what you would like?'' he asked when his face met hers.

''Do it again and I'll let you know.''

This time he started at the hollow of her throat and moved downward, across her shoulders, her chest, and when he got to the valley between her breasts, he stopped, grabbed her hand and pulled her over to a secluded grassy area on the creek bank. ''The butte,'' she whispered.

''What?''

''In the wide open. I want us to be in the wide open, Chay. Just you and me and nothing else.''

Chay zipped up his jeans, and without a word scooped Joanna's wet, naked body up in his arms and carried her up to the top of the butte, then set her gently on the blanket. ''I would have figured you for something more traditional,'' he said, lying down next to her, pulling her into his arms.

''Me, too.'' Reaching down between them, Joanna unzipped and tugged his jeans over his hips this time, wiggling down until she was able to pull them all the way off him. Then she kissed a trail of hot, quick kisses from his toes all the way back to his belly. ''But I was wrong.'' She turned to her side, moving her legs to circle his hips, then pressed herself exuberantly against him, thrusting to feel as much of him against her as she could. ''There's something exciting about being naked in the Big Open, don't you think?''

''You're killing me,'' he groaned, thrusting back at her.

''On your back, Doctor. Apparently, I need to do a physical exam.'' As he turned over, she lowered herself to her knees next to him and bent to kiss her way across his flat stomach, stopping just above his erection. Looking up at him, she asked, ''Where does it hurt?''

Instead of answering, Chay merely sucked in a sharp breath and let out a dull moan.

The sensation of him almost more than she could bear, Joanna pressed harder into Chay, kneading her hands across his chest and all the way down the rippling muscles of his abdomen to feel his imposing hardness, and she lingered there, teasing and taunting and stroking him in order to elicit the moans she was desperate to hear. "I'm almost ready with a diagnosis," she said, following the path of her hands with hard, demanding kisses.

"Skip the diagnosis. I need the cure."

"Believe me, I aim to cure." Joanna lingered over him, teasing every aching spot on his body he was aware of and many he hadn't been before now, until he thought he was going to explode. When he could stand it no longer he sat up, pushed her back onto the blanket and took his place between her legs. Leaning up on his elbows, he looked down, and she almost took his breath away she was so beautiful with the moonlight cascading over her naked body. Stunning, bold and yet almost shy. Not like any woman he'd ever known. And he wanted her so badly it scared him. "And now it's time for me to make *my* diagnosis, Dr Killian."

Chay's hand began the exploration over Joanna's belly then down to that sensitive spot between her legs. "I need a second opinion here, Doctor," he teased, loving the feel of her squirming against his hand. "Is this where you need attention?"

"Chay," she gasped, lifting her hips to his touch. Each stroke, each bold path he traced over her sent an intensifying tremor through her, one after another, until her body finally surrendered a hard climax, one like nothing he'd ever seen before. Joanna was totally abandoned to the moment, to them. To him. To this…whatever it was.

He hadn't expected it to go this far. And he was already

beginning to feel the dull throb of unslaked desire as he pulled back from her. Damn it, anyway. He'd known before he'd started he couldn't finish. Shouldn't have started, actually. But he couldn't help it. Not with Joanna.

"Chay?" she asked. "What's wrong?"

"I, um, I'm not prepared to go any further." True words in so many ways.

"I'm on the Pill," she said.

No, he moaned inwardly as she moved to her knees. He wanted to resist. Tried resisting. But as she pushed him backward there was nothing about him that even suggested resistance. "Are you sure about this?" he asked, moving to let her straddle him.

In answer, Joanna rose up slightly, then lowered herself over him. "I trust you," she said. "Completely." When all of him was in her, she remained still for a moment, and the look of her there atop him, her breasts outlined against the dim night light, made him realize that there was nothing he could deny her. Or wanted to deny her.

"And I'm sure," she whispered as she began to rock slowly up and down on him.

Their rhythm came slowly at first, then finally in a delirious beat that sought its release immediately. Joanna thrust harder and harder against him, driving herself downward for everything he had, until he could control it no longer. This was the sweet release he needed, and only from Joanna. They climaxed together in a frenzy of night-time heat and sweat and hungry gasps.

"So what's your diagnosis, Doctor?" he asked after her last shudder was spent and she was snuggled into his arms.

"Pending further examination, I say perfect. And your diagnosis, Doctor?"

"I think I'll need to schedule you for a recheck," he whispered. What he really wanted to tell her was that it was better than perfect and so much more than he'd ever expected. But he couldn't, and he refused to think beyond that because the reasons scared him. Instead, he pulled Joanna even closer to him, and they clung together naked in the Montana night, without another word between them.

As the night crept on, they returned to the creek to cool down, to find their clothes, then they made their way back to reality.

"It says I need to go back to Rising Sun right away." Joanna couldn't tell him that the note tacked to her door when they returned to the makeshift clinic said that his father had collapsed earlier. To begin with, she didn't know how to tell him, whether he'd care, whether he'd disregard it. And she did so want him to care, but she was afraid to put it to the test because if he didn't, she didn't know how she'd feel about that. She already had a certain image of Chay built up, and in it he did care. Besides, there was no indication about Leonard's condition in the note other than he was resting at home presently. So there was no reason to worry Chay over this yet. "Why don't you stay here tonight? I'll be back in the morning. No need for both of us to go all the way back there."

"Why don't I drive so we can get there faster, and get back here faster?"

Grabbing clean clothes from her duffel bag, ones that looked like they hadn't been discarded along a creek for an evening of what they'd done together, Joanna also pulled out some panties. House calls without underwear didn't seem right. "I'll be fine. And this way, one of us will get some sleep so we can get to our...*my* calls tomorrow." It was already so easy having him there as part of her practice, she found herself slipping into the habit. A very insecure habit to get herself into. And out of.

"You sleep, I'll drive." He grinned, unzipping his jeans to make a quick change, too. "I'll sleep later, while you're being the doctor.'' Without a hint of modesty between them, Chay slipped out of his clothes and walked across the tiny living quarters buck naked to retrieve his own duffel. As much as she would have loved to linger and watch, she couldn't think about that while his dad was sick. So Joanna took that opportunity to slip into the tiny stall bathroom and make her change. When she came out, he was waiting. Fresh jeans, boots, T-shirt, hat. So gorgeous she ached just from the sight of him.

Amazing how she'd never come even close to that kind of a reaction with the man she'd gone so far as to marry.

''Joanna, wake up. We're almost there. You need to tell me where we're going.''

Joanna opened her eyes surprised to find they were already back in Rising Sun. Punching the light on her wristwatch, she was even more surprised at how quickly they'd arrived. ''How fast did you drive?'' she asked.

''Fast enough. So tell me where we're going before we waste all the time I made up.''

The trip all the way to the clinic to drop him off would take ten more minutes, then the trip back out this way, to the Ducheneaux home, would take another ten. No choice. ''Your place,'' she said. ''Your dad collapsed earlier this evening.''

Chay made a sharp cut off the road onto a dirt path, then turned off that in a matter of seconds and headed out though the wilds. ''Why the hell didn't you tell me?'' he snarled, swerving to avoid a stump that seemed to jump into the headlights.

Joanna banged up against the door of the Jeep and her seat belt locked tight over her chest. Struggling to loosen it, she braced herself for the rough, off-road ride ahead. ''Because Leonard's not your patient, and even out here I respect doctor-patient confidentiality.''

"Damn it, Joanna. He's my father. I have a right to know."

"You do, from him, if he decides to tell you. But that's not my decision." The Jeep went airborne over a small hill and thudded to the ground just beyond it, jarring her from her toes to her eyeballs. "Would you slow down?" she yelled. "Getting us both killed won't help your father. And when we get there you can't see him, Chay."

"What do you mean, I can't see him?"

"Do I really have to answer that?" She could see the lights of the Ducheneaux house in the distance. They lived central to both Rising Sun and the ranch. And pretty much nowhere. There wasn't another soul around for a mile, unless the prairie dogs counted. It's so lonely out here, she thought as they pulled up in front of the house. Especially for Wenona, at a time like this. "You take care of your mother, and I'll take care of your father."

Chay didn't say a word as he leapt from the Jeep and ran to the front porch. She expected to find him at Leonard's bedside by the time she got in there but, thank heavens, as Joanna rushed in the door, Chay was already sitting on the sofa, holding his mother in his arms.

"Take care of him Joanna," he whispered over Wenona's sobs. "I trust you. Completely."

She understood the look on his face. It was one seen on every good physician at the moment of a life-or-death situation. It was the one on her own face just last month as she'd signed the order to discontinue Jack Whirlwind's ventilator then had watched Phyllis sitting at his bedside holding his hand, talking to him until the very end. Yes, she understood the look on Chay's face, just as he understood the nod she gave him as she rushed into Leonard's room.

She would do her best, but there were never any promises.

CHAPTER EIGHT

"LEONARD?" Joanna moved quietly to his bedside and looked down at him. "Leonard, can you hear me? It's DocJo." She took his hand and held it. "If you can hear me, squeeze my hand."

He didn't.

Leonard Ducheneaux was very pallid. Pallid and nearly lifeless, Joanna discovered quickly. His pulse was thready and rapid. Breathing fast and labored. "Leonard, I know you don't go for my kind of medicine, but Wenona is worried about you, and she called me." Pulling out her blood-sugar meter, one of the first things she always did for an unknown problem, she slipped in the test strip, lanced his finger and squeezed out a droplet of blood. Several seconds later she had her answer. The reading was well over eight hundred.

Diabetes for sure. A coma, and she suspected a stroke on top of it. His pupils were not reactive. His face was drawn up a little on the left side. It happened like this, especially to people who had long years of untreated diabetes behind them. Unfortunately for Leonard, he was well past his golden hour, when the effects of a stroke often could be substantially reversed. But the chances were, his diabetes was so wildly out of control nothing could have reversed the stroke anyway. "OK, Leonard. I've got to get you to the hospital for some more tests." And soon. Another spike in blood sugar or another stroke could, and probably would, kill him.

Chay was still holding his mother when Joanna returned to the living room. She could feel his eyes burning into her as she walked on through without a word to him, and went directly to the phone. This was the hard part. *I'm sorry. He's in a diabetic coma and he's had a stroke. Both conditions are killing him.* How could she tell them that? Damn, how she hated the bad news.

At least Leonard would warrant a helicopter. "I've got a bad one," she whispered to the dispatcher, hoping Wenona and Chay wouldn't overhear. This wasn't the way they needed to find out. "Rising Sun. Diabetic coma, stroke. He's holding on, but not for long."

"How long?" Chay asked, stepping up behind her.

She whirled around to face him. "Where's your mother?"

"In with my dad."

"I don't know, Chay. His glucose tops out at over eight hundred, and I think—"

"With a stroke, secondary to his diabetes."

He said that so matter-of-factly he could have been reading from a medical textbook rather than enquiring about his father, and that sent an icy chill up Joanna's spine. "He's past the point of trying a thrombolytic." Thrombolytics were commonly called clot-busters because if administered in time they had the potential to break up the blood clot that had caused the stroke, restore normal circulation and in some cases reverse the damage already done. Only, in Leonard's case, it was much too late. Thrombolytics were effective at the early onset of the stroke and the later after the incident they were administered, the less likely they were to work. Leonard was beyond that stage now because he'd been ill for hours. Actually, she guessed he'd been ill for months, maybe years, and the stroke had merely been his body's final way of telling him it could no longer endure, that it was giving up.

"Did you give him insulin?"

"No, he needs better control with that than anything I can do here."

"So you're just going to let his blood sugar keep going up until, what? He dies?"

"Normally, you support the stroke first, then deal with the blood sugar. I wasn't here to support the stroke so there's no sense talking about that because what's done is done. And another hour with his elevated blood sugar isn't going to make him any worse than he already is right now." She was trying to keep her voice low so Wenona wouldn't hear. "Too rapid a correction may cause electrolyte and acid-base changes, which will make things worse for him— maybe cause some kind of cardiac episode. And to be honest, I don't have what it takes to get him back if he goes bad. So he's hanging in there for now, and I think the best thing to do for your father is wait until we can get him someplace that can manage both situations." She reached out and took Chay's hand, half expecting him to pull away from her, but he didn't. In fact, he pulled her into his arms.

"I'm sorry," he whispered. "You know more about this than I do."

"I'm sorry, Chay. I wish I'd known. Maybe I could have—"

"Not with my father you couldn't have. He's stubborn."

"Just like his son."

"Chay?"

Joanna looked up to see Wenona standing in the door. So solemn and pale, she was still as steady as a rock. "We're going to take your husband to Billings in just a little while," Joanna said, pulling out of Chay's arms. "He's stable enough for the trip, and I don't have what he needs here."

Wenona nodded, and Joanna suspected she knew, and understood, far more than anyone gave her credit for. Her husband had been sick for a long time, sick and stubborn and holding on to his traditions, and Wenona had been forced to stand back and watch. What an awful thing for her. Watching, knowing, understanding, and not able to help.

"Chay, is this the best way for your father?" Wenona asked.

He nodded. "The only way. I promise."

Joanna saw the muscle tighten in Chay's jaw, saw him ball his fist. But she also saw him look at his mother with so much love it brought tears to her eyes. She might have looked at her own mother that way, or her father. She hoped she had. But she didn't remember.

"I'm glad you're here. You will do the right thing." Wenona smiled, nodding. "And no matter what has happened between you and your father, you have never let me down." Wenona shuffled past him then returned to wait with her husband until the helicopter arrived.

"I'm surprised she didn't ask you to do something like your father did for Michael Red Elk. Could you? Would it help, do you think?"

"An extraction? I could, but from me it would do him no good. It takes two, and both of them have to believe. My father would believe *nothing* from me, and my mother knows that. And I'm not sure I believe. Not sure I ever believed in those ways."

"But you're a shaman."

"Yeah, well, what's in a title? It wasn't my choice, Joanna. When I was sixteen and my father determined that I was a shaman, the next in the lineage, he took me to the sweat lodge to initiate me. *Inipi*. The rite of purification. It's supposed to utilize all the powers of the universe in order to make you a better person. The earth and the things that grow from it—water, fire, air. There's a round fireplace in the center of the lodge, and we were supposed to sit around it and contemplate how all those elements related to the universe. But you know what? All I could contemplate was a date with Mary Lejeune. She was gorgeous, I was young, horny, and so close to getting it from her. And I didn't give a damn about much of anything else. Including contemplating the mysteries of the universe. But you've got to contemplate those things if you want to purify yourself, because the belief is that the power of any thing, or any act, is found in understanding it. We sat in the sweat lodge, a sauna, if you will, with its fire going, and contemplated and prayed. Sweat, prayer, and some peyote from time to time. That was the cool stuff, because it made the hours that came after it bearable. And I hated it, Joanna. My father's prayers were for worthiness. Mine were for finding a way out of there.

"When it was over my father said I was born a new man, but I think he knew. He took me through the rituals, and I think he hoped for me, but I also think he knew."

"And you never believed in some great power or whatever it was your father was trying to teach you?"

"In the sweat lodge?" He laughed bitterly. "You've got to be kidding. They took my grandfather in there when I was ten, to heal him through purification. Then they buried him. After that, the sweat lodge scared the hell out of me. And the only thing that got me through it was thinking about Mary Lejeune. That, among an awful lot of other impure thoughts."

"But you respected your father enough to sit with him through it, maybe even fake it."

"Yeah, I did. And you know what? He didn't respect me enough to stand by me when I went to medical school."

"There are a lot of ways to heal and be healed, Chay. Whether it's through medicine or surgery, an extraction, a purification, or simply talking. You're dad's a sick man and I certainly wouldn't rule out any of them for him."

Joanna stood on tiptoe to kiss Chay gently on the cheek, then she went back to wait with Wenona and Leonard.

Chay stayed in the kitchen and fixed himself a cherry cola.

*   *   *

Joanna hated helicopters. The only thing she'd actually ever enjoyed off solid ground had been her little tryst up on the butte. And already that seemed so long ago. Especially right now as she snapped on her helmet and fastened herself in for the ride.

Flying in a helicopter was a lot like riding in one of those great express elevators in the fifty-story hotels. First came the trip straight up, and that was never too bad because she imagined a beautiful penthouse at the top of her journey. But then eventually that elevator would start to move forward as well as continue its ascent, and that's where the fantasy stopped for her. Because at about a thousand feet off the ground, that smooth-riding elevator started careening through the air at a hundred miles per hour. Nothing in her life ever went that fast, including her heart after her evening on the butte, and in the creek, with Chay. And if ever there was a time that something in her life should have been flying that fast, that had been it.

Now she was a thousand feet up, flying over nowhere in the dark, praying that Leonard would remain stable for the trip, because if he didn't, the casual-looking paramedic sitting across from her eating his dinner might actually expect something from her. Something other than panic, which was the only thing she would ever guarantee when she was forced into one of these flights.

Chay was driving to Billings, taking his mother and his grandmother. She thought about him for a moment as she reached to take Leonard's pulse. Chay tried so desperately to act dispassionately. On the surface it was a good front. But she'd seen the look in his eyes when he'd found out about his dad, and there had been no dispassion there. None at all. "You're a stubborn man," she whispered to Leonard, despite the noise of the helicopter motor and even though he probably couldn't hear her. "So is Chay. And you're both wrong. Do you hear me, Leonard? You're both wrong.''

The flight medic smiled over at her, acknowledging something that he, like Leonard, hadn't heard.

''When are you going to give up whatever it is you're doing out there and come practice real medicine?'' Greg Reynolds, the emergency department attending physician slid his arms around Joanna's waist—a familiar advance she was used to from him, and more often than not ignored. ''I've got a spot open for you any time you want it.''

''I'll just bet you do,'' she replied, disengaging herself from him. Greg had been trying for some sort of relationship almost from the moment she'd stepped foot in Montana. He was a good doctor, but terrible in the personal relationship department. Rumor had him sleeping with most of the emergency nurses and female doctors at one time or another. Maybe some women found the fair-haired, slick-looker attractive, but lately she'd been much more interested in the dark, rugged, brooding kind. ''And I still like what I'm doing out there. I will the next time you ask me, too.''

''Joanna and the coyotes. You'll be changing your mind about that, and I'll be waiting right here with open arms when you do.'' He tossed her a sly little wink. ''And I'll guarantee that I'll be much better company than the coyotes.''

Actually, she'd prefer the coyotes, but she needed to stay on Greg's good side because over the months he'd become an ally to her. He took care of her emergencies, and as often as not looked the other way when the paperwork and regulations threatened to get in the way of patient care. He bent rules for her, and she needed that. Her patients needed that. ''You just keep those arms open for me, Greg, because you never know.'' She blew him a mock kiss then scooted on into the cubicle where Leonard was hooked up to a slow infusion of insulin. An hour in treatment now, and he was looking better. Not so gray. Vital signs stable. Last blood-sugar reading, however, had shown him on the decline.

"He's not responsive," the nurse told her. "His pupils are equal and reactive, but he's not coming round." The nurse, a cute, tomboyish brunette who looked more like a kid than an adult, hooked the chart over the foot of the bed and left the area.

Joanna picked it up and read. CAT scan negative for bleeding. That was good. Blood gases within normal range, and except for his blood sugar the rest of his labs were essentially within normal limits, too. Actually, except for the fact that Leonard Ducheneaux had let his diabetes go so badly out of control that it had caused a stroke, he was fine. Well, fine enough under the circumstances, since the kidney work-ups were yet to be done, and kidneys often suffered minor to total damage from unchecked diabetes. Leonard, she noted, was puffy in his extremities, which meant his kidneys might be fighting him on top of everything else that was wrong.

"Could it have been the flu vaccine that brought this on?" she asked Greg, who'd stepped into the cubicle with her.

"Probably not. This guy's been dodging the big one for a long time, from the looks of his lab work. A1C's sky-rocketing at twelve, meaning the guy's averaging three times his normal blood-sugar level. Which leads me right to the neuropathy I found on his right leg." Neuropathy meant the circulation in Leonard's legs was compromised and some of the tissue and nerve function were essentially dying. Best-case scenario was surgery to restore normal circulation, worst case came in two varieties. Gangrene, if not treated, which would lead to amputation or death. And amputation, if treated and circulation still could not be restored.

"How bad?" Diabetic neuropathy scared her. She'd already seen two below-the-knee amputations since she'd been on Hawk, and twice that many amputated toes. Just the word "neuropathy" made her blood run cold.

"It's not severe yet, and I think we can probably take care of it with surgery. I hope. But if he's not careful he's going to be up for some chopping. And about his kidneys, well, heaven only knows what's going on there since we're not getting enough normal urinary output at present to judge. We've got him on some Lasix to kick out the fluid, but if that doesn't work then we're going to look at some kind of dialysis maybe. Hemodialysis if it's bad, peritoneal if he's lucky. So, could it have been the flu vaccine? I doubt it. If you gave it to him today, I'd say it was a coincidence on top of someone who was going to crash anyway. Oh, and I'm going to line him up for vascular, neurology, nephrology and endocrinology consults later today."

For someone who avoided modern medicine, Leonard was about to see more than his fair share of it. Poor Leonard, Joanna thought, pulling Greg into the hall. "Even with all that, is he going to make it?"

"Don't know, Jo. It's too soon to tell, and there are so many elements here that can go wrong. But even if he recovers, he's going to need a lot of physical therapy. I mean, your patient has a damn long road ahead of him if he pulls out of the crisis. I'm not sure he's going to, and if he does, who knows if he's going to work hard enough to keep himself alive?" Greg took a deep breath, regrouped and continued, "Sorry. That came out the wrong way. I want him to recover, of course. I want him to go home and live a long and happy life, and I shouldn't have said what I did, but it's so damned frustrating. You fix them up, send them home, then the next time they come back in worse condition than they were in the time before. I see it every day. Same faces, same conditions. Makes me mad as hell, Jo.''

''Me, too, Greg. Believe me, I fight it as hard as you do, and I still lose.''

''Is he more than a patient? A friend or something?''

''A friend of a friend.'' She glanced down the corridor behind Greg at Chay, who was heading toward them. ''And it's OK, what you said. I've been on Hawk six months and Leonard never once came to me even though he knows he's been sick.''

''Tough job. I hope they're not all like that out there.''

Joanna smiled. ''You mean stubborn? Thank God, no. Most of the people want more medical care than I can give them, and they try hard, within their means, to do what they're supposed to. Leonard just happens to be one of the very few stubborn ones who stick to the old ways. Look, do me a favor here and let me talk to his family. OK? I know Leonard's under your care now, but...''

Greg gave her a sly wink. ''I'll just put it on the list of things you'll be owing me for later on.'' He leaned in close to her ear, whispering, ''And how about we make that sooner rather than later? You and me, someplace dark and cozy like my—''

''Dr Ducheneaux,'' Joanna interrupted as Chay stepped up. Just in the nick of time! ''This is Dr Reynolds.'' She forced a sweet smile on Greg. ''Dr Ducheneaux is Leonard's son.''

The handshake between the men was curt, then as Greg pulled away, he asked, ''Doctor, as in what? Medicine?''

''Voodoo,'' Chay snapped, slipping into Leonard's cubicle.

''Orthopedic surgeon,'' Joanna said, seizing the opportunity to get away from Greg and follow Chay. She stayed at the entry for a moment, watching them—Leonard on the bed, so still and helpless, Chay standing over it, staring at the monitors and not his father. ''He might be able to hear if you talk to him,'' she said.

''He hasn't wanted to hear me for half my life, and I don't think that's going to change now.''

As Chay spoke, Joanna saw a barely detectable increase in Leonard's heart rate blip across the cardiac monitor. Just a few beats more per minute, and once Chay quit speaking, Leonard's heart rate dropped back down to where it had been. ''He's sick, Chay. That changes things.''

''With others maybe. But not him.''

Leonard's heart rate went up and down again. ''And not you either, apparently.'' Chay spun around to face her and for a moment she thought she saw a flash of anguish cross his face, but if she had, it disappeared almost as quickly as it had appeared. What was left was the stone-cold expression she saw only when it came to his father. ''How about we go outside and talk while they move him to MICU?'' she suggested. The medical intensive care unit. ''I'd like to see Wenona and Macawi for a few minutes, too, and let them know what's going to be happening to Leonard throughout the night.'' She motioned Chay over to her, then whispered, ''Before you leave, go tell your father that you'll be back to see him in a little while. Will you do that for me?''

He shrugged his blatant indifference, then returned to Leonard's side. ''Look, they're going to get you settled into a room, so I'm going to go wait with Mom and Macawi. But I'll be back later.''

Joanna's eyes were fixed on the monitor. Leonard's rate went from sixty-eight to eighty-two. ''He can hear you, Chay. He knows you're here and he's listening to you.''

Two hours after Leonard was admitted to the MICU and Wenona and Macawi were settled into the hotel across the street from the hospital—settled in with great protest since MICU visiting hours were ten minutes every other hour and wouldn't start up again for several hours—Joanna and Chay were heading back to Rising Sun against the backdrop of the rising sun. It was a magnificent view, Joanna thought, driving and sipping coffee to keep herself awake while Chay slumped in the seat next to her and stared out the window. Magnificent, awe-inspiring. This place called the Big Open was deep in her heart now. Maybe it was the only place in which she'd ever been truly happy.

"I told him he needed to be seen," Chay said, after nearly an hour of silence. "Told him yesterday morning, for all the good it did."

"You can't force someone to get help if they don't want to. I'm sure you did the best you could."

"Yeah." He snorted. "I pushed him in the opposite direction."

"The world doesn't revolve around you, Chay. Not even this little piece of it. Your father made his choice, and it had nothing to do with you. It was a choice he made months, probably even years ago. Without any regard to you, I'm betting. But if you want to sit there and soak up all that guilt, blame yourself for his choices, his mistakes, be my guest. Help yourself to it. Just leave me out of it, OK? Because I've got a hundred more just like your dad waiting to happen. And they, Dr Ducheneaux, aren't your fault, just like your dad isn't."

"And they're not your fault either," he said quietly, reaching over to give her hand a squeeze.

Kind words. Too kind, as it turned out, because they were the words that opened a locked door, one she'd tried so hard to keep locked since she'd realized that no matter what she did on Hawk, no matter how hard she worked, it would never be enough. "But it is my fault," she said, swiping at the tears that were already beginning to fall. "I'm not enough, Chay, and they all suffer for that. As hard as I try, I can't do it." Before the good, hard crying hit, Joanna swerved off the road, hopped out of the Jeep, and headed out into the prairie, no destination in mind other than away from where she was. She would fight it, walk it off, not let it get her. But after only a minute it gripped her anyway, and she tumbled to the ground for the soul-wrenching, gut-wrenching cry she'd wanted since her first day there.

But she didn't cry alone. Not as she'd thought she would. She cried in Chay's arms until there were no more tears and the only thing left was that magnificent rising sun.

And the man with whom she was falling in love. The man for whom, like the people of Hawk who were entrusted to her care, she could never be enough.

CHAPTER NINE

"TELL me exactly what they told you," Chay said over the phone to Wenona. He'd called the hospital twice today already and had heard the same thing: critical but stable. Which told him nothing. His dad was sick, possibly dying, and holding steadily on that precipice. Chay knew he would have to go back there soon to take care of his mother and Macawi.

Few words were exchanged between Chay and his mother. She sounded tired, he thought. Tired, but determined to fight the fight for her husband. And she didn't want to stay away from the waiting room too long for fear one of the doctors or nurses had something to report on Leonard's condition and she would miss it. So he listened to his mother recount what the doctors had said, then retold it to her in terms a non-medical person would understand.

"His blood sugar stabilizing means that his diabetes is coming under his control, which is good. Urinary output picking up with Lasix means his kidneys are working better." That one was a big relief. The little bit of urine he'd seen in the collection bag had worried him more than just about everything else. Kidney failure in an area without services was tantamount to death—the sad truth Phyllis Whirlwind was now dealing with. "And a guarded neurological status doesn't really say much. They're waiting to see how badly the stroke has injured him and they won't know until he wakes up."

His dad had been in the coma so many hours now. Chay glanced at the clock on Joanna's kitchen wall. Almost twenty-four hours, and that wasn't a good sign. The longer he stayed comatose the more his odds of serious, maybe even permanent impairment increased. So, all told, critical but stable. Something akin to Joanna's condition, only hers was emotional. She suffered the price each and every one of her patients paid, and holding her all night, as he'd done, had been much, *much* too little, considering what she needed. He'd thought about that as she slept, thought about it, then resisted the way the answers were starting to line up. This was a fling, for heaven's sake. By definition a casual affair, a period of self-indulgence. But no matter how he tried reframing it, and he'd tried, nothing about what he had going with Joanna came close to casual or self-indulgent. Which was why he'd spent the night thinking about her needs and not his own.

"Look, Mom, I'll talk to you again in a couple of hours, and if you need anything in the meantime, call me. Will you do that, Mom?"

He hung up when he was convinced his mother would call him, and went back to Joanna's bed. She'd slept all day, and now, well into the evening, she was still sleeping. Chay debated climbing back in with her, holding her, waking up with her. But he was restless, too restless to confine himself, and the walls were certainly beginning to close in on him. Part of him wanted to go back to Chicago, forget that he'd ever been here, write his mother a check for his dad's medical care so he could pretend to be the dutiful son without feeling the strain of real involvement. But so much more of him wanted to be here. For his mother and Macawi in the widest sense, maybe even for his dad a little, which was something he needed to figure out. Most of all, he wanted to be here for Joanna, which sure as hell didn't fit into any kind of plans he had for himself.

Chay wandered over to his mother's diner. It was closed now, but he knew how to get in the back window. A trick left over from his childhood. The only reason he'd even gone in after hours had been for a cherry cola. It was like a balm that seemed to cure everything. Funny how in all the years he'd been away he'd never had one. And now he wanted one so badly he was willing to squeeze his man-sized frame through a window that better accommodated a boy just to get it.

Once in, he headed to the soda fountain, stopping to look at the framed pictures on the walls. All pictures of people from Rising Sun enjoying themselves in the diner. So many of the faces he recognized—Ralph Bird from the garage. He was smiling as he was photographed eating what was probably a bowl of ham and beans. And there was Wendy Godenot diving into a banana split. Chay walked slowly along Wenona's wall of fame until he came to the one where he and Jack Whirlwind were looking like a couple of gawky geeks drinking their cherry cola out of a bucket. They'd been going fishing that day, and instead of a Thermos, which would have been the sensible thing to fill up, they'd dragged in a big old galvanized bucket. What were they? Twelve years old maybe? Back when life was simple, futures were simple. They would grow up and work on the ranch as their fathers and grandfathers had, and go fishing on Saturdays.

"Yeah, right," Chay grunted, reaching out to touch the face of his friend. "Back when things were simple, Jack. So what the hell happened to us?" Chay shut his eyes, trying to block out the memories, but they wouldn't be blocked. He'd been happy here once. But that life had gotten away from him. "So tell me, Jack. If I'd come home after med school, would it have made a difference? Would you still be alive? Would my dad be…?" Chay spun away from the wall of fame and headed to the soda fountain. "Hell," he muttered, fishing the customary dime out of his pocket and plunking it down on the counter next to the cash register.

One cherry cola poured, Chay sat down at the counter to drink it, but two sips into it he was interrupted by a tapping on the window. Since everybody knew Wenona's closed after mid-afternoon, he decided to keep his back to the window, ignore whoever wanted in. But the tapping persisted until he finally glanced back to see the face of Kimimela pressed to the window. She was crying.

Chay opened the door to let her in, and she flew into his arms. "I can't find my mommy," she wailed. "She said she would come home to fix my supper, but she didn't."

"Where's your daddy?" Chay asked, lifting her to the stool where he'd sat and sliding his cherry cola toward her.

"Don't got one."

"Was someone looking after you while your mother went out?"

"I can look after myself," she said, almost defiantly. "Did you pay a dime for that?" she asked, before she took the drink.

"I most certainly did. That's the rule. So, Little Butterfly, did your mommy tell you where she was going?"

She shook her head, sniffling back a second round of tears.

"Do you know any friends she likes to visit in the evening?"

Kimimela shook her head again. "She has lots of friends but they don't come to our house."

"Well, how about we take that drink with us and go back to your house? I'll bet your mother's probably home now, wondering where you are." As he took Kimimela's hand and led her out the door, he wondered about a mother who would let such a young child stay home alone. Maybe that was his Chicago ways coming through. He remembered his own freedom at a young age, freedom no child in a big city should ever have because it wasn't safe there. And certainly there had been many nights such as this when he'd gone out on his own, as Kimimela had done. Of course, he remembered his dad waiting for him at the door on most of those nights. Big, imposing sight, arms folded across his chest, frowning. Just the sight of his dad standing there like that had been enough of a punishment. But Leonard had always had something else in mind: a restriction from something Chay enjoyed—television, a town baseball game, cherry cola. "So you came to the diner looking for your mother?" he asked Kimimela.

"Looking for you, DocChay. I knew my mother wouldn't be here. She doesn't like to come here when she doesn't have to. She likes to go to that other place where they have music. Sometimes she dances there and gets paid."

The roadhouse out by the ranch. Popular place for a lot of the ranch hands. Pool tables, booze, women. A very popular place for the men who didn't go home to their wives at night. "OK. Why don't you take me to your house to see if your mom has come home? Maybe she's there waiting for you right now." Although somehow he didn't think so.

Kimimela's house was a short walk, about two blocks. It was a small, run-down wood frame house, probably with only two rooms, and Chay knocked several times before he decided that no one was home. "Well, Little Butterfly, it looks like you're right. No one's home. So, do you have a grandmother or an aunt who lives here?"

"Uh-uh. Just Mommy and me."

"Then how about we go give DocJo a visit?" After that, what? Go look for Kimimela's mother, or wait until her mother remembered she had a child at home?

Joanna had half expected to find Chay in bed with her, but she wasn't terribly surprised to find him gone. They'd had a tumultuous twenty-four hours, and he'd probably gone off somewhere to think about what they were doing. They'd made love at Fishback Creek—and she was going to call it making love because for her that was what it had been, even if for him it had probably been just sex on a butte with someone who'd been willing. And she had been. Then after the creek, the way he'd held her out on the prairie and on through the night when everything had come apart for her. His arms around her for an hour as she'd cried, then as she'd simply lingered there to search for a bit of calmness and control in her life. And then the way they'd lain spoon-fashion all night. She fit right into him, and it had been a natural thing to do, one that had seemed like they'd done it many times before. With so much crammed into such a short time frame, she wasn't surprised he wasn't there, but she was a bit disappointed. Waking up in Chay's arms would have been so wonderful.

Joanna climbed out of bed and plodded to the shower, thinking about all the possibilities between them. Realistically, she wasn't going to keep him there. But Chicago wasn't that far away, and she was accumulating quite a bit of time off, as she hardly ever took the days off coming to her. And maybe, if his feelings toward her were more than casual, and she prayed they were, he might come back for occasional visits. Especially now that his family needed him.

One moment at a time—that was the way it was going to be. Take one moment, be glad for it, and not anticipate the next.

Well, one thing was for sure. It wasn't the kind of relationship she'd expected to step into. After her marriage had fallen apart, she hadn't even thought in terms of a relationship of any sort. But right now that was all she was thinking about, even if she couldn't define it in any specific terms other than difficult. "So take it for what it is," she said, stepping into the shower. A light, easy sentiment. Unfortunately, her growing feelings for Chay were anything but light and easy. And that was the problem. A very big problem.

"Joanna?"

She heard the voice over the spray of the shower. "Care to join me?" she called. Probably not appropriate, considering his father's condition. But she'd rung before she'd climbed out of bed and Leonard was still holding his own. Not better, but not worse.

"I need to talk to you."

She poked her head between the shower curtains and was greeted by a scowl she was beginning to know all too well. "Your dad?" she gasped, wondering if something had happened since she'd called.

Chay shook his head. "Kimimela's mother. She's not home and Kimimela's out wandering the streets."

"Give me a minute." Joanna ducked back into the shower, took about a minute to wash, then wrapped herself in a large towel and stepped out. Chay was still standing there, waiting. For just a second she saw a look of appreciation flash across his eyes, but then it was gone and the scowl returned.

"Do you know anything about the woman?" he asked.

"Her name's Donna. She's single, and I don't know anything about Kimi's father. Occasionally Donna dances down at the roadhouse and your mother watches Kimi for the night when she does." Joanna thought about kicking him out of the bathroom while she dried off and dressed, or at the very least asking him to do the gentlemanly thing and turn his back. But instead, amazed by the boldness he inspired in her, she let the towel drop to the floor at his feet.

"Damn," Chay muttered, reaching out to stroke her breasts. "This isn't fair. I've got a kid sitting downstairs, waiting for me, and as much as I'd love to, I can't—"

"Kimi's here?" she sputtered. That changed Joanna's mood abruptly, and she quickly pulled on her bra and panties, the nice, cheeky ones he liked, then grabbed some khaki shorts. "Why didn't you tell me she's here? You can't be in here with me, Chay. Not in the bathroom. Not with Kimi down there."

He didn't budge. Not a step. "I brought her here because where else was I supposed to take her? I left her playing with your stethoscope."

After she pulled on her T-shirt, Joanna shoved around Chay and headed to the bathroom door. Before she opened it, she turned back to him and whispered, "Kimi's mother isn't around much for her. Your mother has been doing most of Kimi's raising since I've been here, and I probably should have reported Donna to child protection services a long time ago, but I haven't because it would break Wenona's heart not to have Kimi around. I guess I never thought that Donna would go off and leave Kimi alone when she knew Wenona wasn't here, but I'm not sure Donna would ever think that far outside herself."

"I think you're right about that," he said softly.

Kimimela was on the examining table in room one, listening through the stethoscope for her brain when Joanna entered. "You can't hear your brain, sweetie," she said, laughing.

"Yes, you can," Kimimela replied in all earnestness. "I hear things going on in it all the time."

"Can't argue with logic like that," Chay said, scooping the little girl up in his arms. "How about we go upstairs and fix you something to eat? By the time your mommy gets home she'll probably be awfully tired."

"Grilled cheese? Mrs Wenona always fixes me grilled cheese."

Chay glanced over at Joanna to make sure she had the ingredients handy in her tiny kitchenette, and when she nodded, he charged at the stairs with Kimimela squealing in his arms. He could have been a pediatrician, Joanna thought. A good one, judging from the way he was with Kimi. A good pediatrician and…a wonderful father.

Just as Joanna turned to follow them up, someone knocked at her door with such a force it almost rattled the frosted inset glass right out of it. She knew that knock, and her heart lurched with the sure recognition of what would come after she opened up. That familiar knock from Emil Chamberlain, one of Hawk's six reservation police officers, never brought good news.

"It's a bad one," he said to Joanna even before the door was fully open. He was winded, overwrought. He also had high blood pressure and Joanna doubted he ever took the medicine she prescribed for him to treat it. "On the way out to the roadhouse, car overturned."

"How many injuries?" she asked.

"Just the one. I sent Joseph Stonehorse over to get her little girl."

Joanna's heart clutched again. "Donna Rousseau?"

Emil nodded. "She'd been drinking, doing some dancing. Some of the guys offered to drive her home but she said she was just going outside for a smoke. Ronnie Fontenoy saw her go off the road. He said she was swerving all over the place, way over the speed limit. Some of the boys are with her, but I told them not to touch her until we talked to you first."

"Give me a minute. Oh, and Chay Ducheneaux's upstairs with Kimi."

"I heard he's back in town. Been meaning to drop by and see him. Look, I'll have someone take Kimi over to Sandy…" He called the words to thin air, because Joanna was already halfway up the stairs.

"Kimi, I've got an emergency and I need DocChay to go with me. But Sheriff Emil's here to take you to his house, and I'll bet his wife, Sandy, can fix you something even better than plain old grilled cheese."

Kimi was agreeable, and within seconds she was sitting in the front seat of the police car, lights and siren on purely for her amusement, while Joanna was sitting next to Chay, who was driving simply because he could get them there faster.

"Donna Rousseau?" he asked as they pulled away from the clinic.

"How did you know?"

"I could see it in your eyes, how sad they were when you looked at Kimimela."

She picked up the radio Emil had left with her and punched a button. "This is Joanna Killian, over." It scared her that Chay was so perceptive, scared her to her very core, because if he could see the depth of her emotions for Kimi, maybe could he also see the depth of her developing feelings for him.

"Joanna, this is Ben Blue Jacket, and I'm sure glad to hear your voice, over."

At times like these she would have traded a year's salary for a cellphone that worked. Unfortunately, they didn't transmit out here. She had one, for all the good it did her, but most of the time her connection was through a land line, and sometimes a radio like this one. "Describe Donna's injuries, over."

"She's crushed under her car, Doc. It turned over and she was thrown out, but it landed on her, over."

"Is she conscious?" She waited for Ben's response.

"Say over," Chay prompted.

"Over," she repeated, numbly.

"She is, and she says she's not feeling a thing. She wants to know if we could take the car off her so she can get on home to Kimi. But it's down hard on her, Doc. Almost like it's buried half of her in the ground, over."

"Vitals, over?"

"Blood pressure's down, heart rate's way up and her breathing is rapid, over."

"Do you keep any oxygen in your patrol car, Ben? Over."

"Sure do, over."

"Get her on some oxygen, and sit tight. We're about ten minutes out. Over. Oh, and, Ben, radio me back if there are any changes at all. Over."

"Shock," Chay said.

It took Joanna a minute to find her voice. If the full weight of the car had crushed Donna and she wasn't feeling anything... No, she wasn't going to buy into the worst-case scenario as she hadn't seen the full extent of the accident. Maybe none of the car had touched Donna at all.

Or maybe all of it had and Donna just didn't know she was dead.

The scene was congested with workers from the ranch when they arrived, and Joanna asked Ben to get rid of everybody. She didn't want Donna going through this with an audience.

"It's serious," Chay said before Joanna even found her way over to the injured woman. "Everything from mid-chest down. She's pinned and happy and drunk, but once we pull the car off she's going to bleed internally and—"

"Options," Joanna snapped. "What are our options? I don't have a MAST suit." MAST—military antishock trousers—were slipped onto a patient in the hope that the pressurized device would increase blood flow to the vital organs, especially the brain and heart, when the patient was suffering a major internal bleed. It was a stopgap measure, often controversial, because it was hard to get on, harder to get off, and it could cause almost as much shock to the system as the initial injury. But in instances such as this, it could work.

Except Joanna didn't have one.

"Wouldn't do any good if you did. Optimum time to keep her in it would be twenty minutes, give or take. And right now that car's acting as the MAST. Once we remove it, if we're not prepared to operate immediately…"

"She'll hemorrhage internally and die." Like the floodgates opening. The car was keeping them shut in a sense, but once opened there was no shutting them again. "So what do we do?" Joanna choked, fighting to keep a grip on her emotions. This was always the hardest part—not being able to do what she was supposed to.

"Make her comfortable, get the chopper here just in case we're wrong, and hope that we are." He reached out and took Joanna's hand. "And do this for her until whatever happens happens."

"Dear God, Chay. I know what it's like to lose your mother at Kimi's age." As much as her heart was breaking for Donna, it was breaking even more for Kimi. And there was nothing Joanna could do to fix it. "Look, you go back to Donna and I'll go talk to Ben Blue Jacket. And don't tell her she's going to die. That might be the coward's way out, but maybe something will happen." Something good, but probably not.

Joanna procrastinated her way over to Donna several minutes later and found Chay sitting with her, holding her hand. How could he do that? she wondered. Sit there so calmly, like it was a first date and they were at a movie? He was such a good doctor, and her heart hurt so badly watching him wait with Donna. Somehow she needed to find the strength for this.

"Donna," Joanna whispered, bending down next to her. Chay was on the other side, his eyes shut. "We have a helicopter on the way for you, and once it's here, we'll get the car off. Are you in much pain?"

"Chayton found my power animal. I've always wondered if I had one and sometimes I was afraid to ask, because maybe I didn't deserve one. But Chayton says it's the horse, that he can feel the spirit of the horse in me, that it's strong.''

Joanna looked over at Chay, but he didn't open his eyes. ''Tell me about the horse, Donna.'' She knew about power animals. Everyone was supposed to have a particular animal, which she thought of as similar to a guardian angel— a protector spirit that helped in daily life and in spiritual search. Power animals were supposed to reflect one's inner self and represent the qualities people needed. They were important in the Sioux spiritual practices and she liked what they represented. Somehow she always thought that if she were to have one, it would be a deer. In Sioux tradition, people whose power animal was a deer were often described as being swift and alert. They were also intuitive, sometimes with well-developed, even extra-sensory perception. Their thoughts seem to race ahead, and often they seemed not to be listening. Like Chay was right now. The deer's medicine was gentleness in word, thought and touch, and the ability to listen, the grace and appreciation for the beauty of balance, understanding what was necessary for survival, power of gratitude and giving, the ability to sacrifice for the higher good. That was the power animal, or guardian spirit, she would have chosen for herself. But she thought it was really the power animal that had chosen Chay.

Donna drew in a deep, shuddering breath. She was beginning to wind down, Joanna saw.

''Chayton says if you have the power of the horse in your spirit, it's difficult to control. I guess you could say that's the way I've lived my life—not under control. But he says I have loyalty and devotion, and I do, DocJo. I love Kimimela, and I've always been devoted to her. I have…'' Her voice trailed off.

''And you have the touch of gypsy in your soul,'' Chay continued for her. ''The horse's medicine brings you the freedom to run where you want.'' He finally looked at Joanna as he spoke the next words to Donna. "A horse will carry you to your freedom, Donna.''

Joanna shut her eyes to hold back the tears.

"Chayton,'' Donna whispered. *"Mic'ikte.'' I killed myself.*

"No, you have freed yourself. *Wakhan Thánka nici um.''* *The Great Spirit will go with you and guide you.*

"And Kimimela?''

"Chéye shni yo.'' Don't cry. "Wash'ake.'' She is strong.

Chay held Donna's hand until she died thirty minutes later, and Joanna was thankful Kimimela's mother had suffered no pain. More than that, she was thankful that Chay had found it within himself to guide Donna Rousseau in the way she should go.

He was indeed the deer.

CHAPTER TEN

It was early morning and she needed to open up the clinic here in Rising Sun as well as get up to Claremont to make up for the missed appointments from…when was it? Only yesterday? Or perhaps the day before? It was all beginning to run together now—the days, the hours, the minutes. So much had happened between getting Leonard to the hospital, and Donna's accident. And now she needed to split herself in half just to catch up. Which meant someone was going to be slighted no matter how she worked it out.

There was also Kimi to consider. Chay wasn't saying anything about what had happened to her mother yet, but he was taking it to heart much more than she had expected him to. Especially since he tried so hard to stay detached.

He'd gone to Billings after Donna had died, to tell his mother firsthand. News like that, on top of her worry over her husband, shouldn't be delivered by phone. Joanna knew she probably should have gone with him, but somebody had to stay back and get the next day started, which was what she was trying to do right now. Fix some coffee, prop her eyes open and greet the patients lining up on the sidewalk outside the clinic.

"Good morning, Mrs Ninon," Joanna said as the first of about a dozen marched through her door. Laurette Ninon, a bit of a hypochondriac, didn't wander too far away from medical services when they were available. Joanna was trying to wean her off, limit her to one visit a week. Of course, these were extenuating circumstances, the aftermath of Donna Rosseau's tragedy. And Laurette had been Donna's friend.

125

"I'm so nervous I don't know what to do with myself, DocJo," Laurette said, sniffling into a tissue. "I'm thinking that Hank and I should do the right thing by Kimimela and take her in like a daughter. That's what Donna would want, I think. But Hank's gone more now, as Leonard's in the hospital. He's trying to take over some of the responsibility at the ranch, which means I'm home alone much more, and since I already have three children…"

Laurette was struggling to keep in the sobs. In fact, there was a dark pall over everyone waiting to see Joanna this morning, and she wasn't looking forward to dealing with it so many times. After Jack Whirlwind's death last month, she'd prayed she wouldn't have to go through it again for a long, long time. And here it was all over again. The people of Rising Sun, and on the whole of the Hawk reservation, were tight-knit. They cared. They pitched in to help one another. They shared lives. And there would be many who, like Laurette, needed consolation.

"I have some sample tranquilizers," Joanna said to Laurette. Truth was, Laurette needed tender loving care more than medication, but there simply wasn't time for TLC, so a low-dose pill was the best she could do. She handed Laurette a sample packet of Valium, 2.5 milligrams a child's dose really. Then a paper cup of water to wash down the pill. It wasn't much, but she was hoping for some placebo effect to kick in. "Now, go home, take the day off rest. And call your mother to come over and watch the kids Doctor's orders."

It was more of a patch job than a real fix, but Laurette took it to heart and thanked her with a wonderful pot o fresh vegetable stew and five one-dollar bills. And that was pretty much how the first half of Joanna's day went. Patch jobs for the most part. A few minor ailments, and so much grieving.

"My dad's beginning to come round," Chay announced

as he strolled into the clinic. It was mid-afternoon and the last of Joanna's patients had finally gone. At the moment she was trying to catch up on paperwork, the one part of her job she really hated. "Doctor says he's responding to verbal stimuli, but he's not totally cognizant of everything around him. My mother thinks he understands everything, though, and I'm going to have to go with what she thinks."

Joanna glanced up from her laptop to look at him. He was tired, too. And still so handsome. That night in Fishback Creek seemed so long ago now she was beginning to question if she'd really been with him or had merely dreamed it. How could so much have happened in such a short time? she asked herself. In the moments when she'd lain in his arms afterward, she'd thought about the next time with him, wondering *when*? Not if. But now she wondered *if*, and she wasn't holding out much hope for it. There were so many other things to come between them, and he would leave soon. "They want to move him to a rehab facility in a few days, Chay, and the best I can do is get him into a place there in Billings." The best she could do, but not nearly good enough.

"My mother wants to bring him home and care for him." Chay pulled up a chair and sat down across from Joanna. "She thinks she and Macawi can take care of whatever he needs."

"I don't want to be blunt about this, Chay, but your mother has watched him being sick for a long time and didn't do anything about it. She didn't even mention it to me, not that I could have done anything. But maybe I could have. Who knows? So I'm not sure, when the time comes for your dad to leave the hospital, if coming home is the best thing. Right away, anyway. Maybe later…"

She looked at the blur of words and figures on her computer screen. Where there were financial subsidies from the government, such as the ones her clinic received, there were always financial reports to file. But she wasn't in the mood. "Have you gone over to see Kimi yet? I talked to Sandy earlier and they haven't told her about Donna. She and Emil thought maybe you should be the one, since you're who she came looking for."

"Yeah, and she'll form some sort of attachment to me, then what?" He stretched back in the chair and crossed one leg over the other. "It was hard enough sitting with Donna."

"I didn't have a chance to tell you what a wonderful thing you did out there, holding her hand, staying with her, helping her through it."

"And then she died," he snapped. "Yeah. Wonderful job. And now Kimimela's an orphan. Damn wonderful."

"What's your power animal, Chay?"

He didn't even look at her. Instead, he dropped his head backward against the wall and shut his eyes. "Don't have one. And don't start on me about what you heard out there with Donna. It was what she needed. That's all. I couldn't save her life, so that's all I had to give her. And don't go getting any crazy idea that I'm having a change of heart, because I'm not. I'm a doctor, a surgeon, and I was taking care of a patient the only way I knew how."

"And that's the point, Chay. You knew how." Joanna pushed away from her desk and stood. "Somebody needs to talk to Kimi. Why don't you go get some sleep and I'll go over to the Chamberlains' and tell Kimi what happened to her mother? By now I'm sure she knows something's wrong."

Chay drew in a ragged breath and let it out slowly. "How about we both go?" He stood up, then pulled her into his arms. "Normally when I ask a girl to go to bed with me it's for things other than sleep, but maybe after we talk to Kimimela we could come back here, take a nice, relaxing bath together then crawl into bed.'' He brushed a light kiss across her lips. "And take a nap.''

"Just what I was about to suggest.''

Chay was simply too tired to figure out his feelings for Joanna right now but, damn it, something was stirring up in him, and it went far beyond what they'd found for themselves at Fishback Creek. The sex had been great, and hopefully what happened wouldn't be a one-night stand for them. But something else was going on, something he couldn't make sense of yet. In the midst of everything else, his ability to think straight had vanished, and when it came to Joanna Killian, he really needed some straight thinking before he tried to sort out what he was feeling for her. Otherwise he'd merely tumble into her arms right then and never, ever leave.

But that wasn't the *real* Chayton Ducheneaux thinking that. Couldn't be. So it must be the delirium, the exhaustion, the emotional whirling that was sucking away his normal responses. Because in the low points—and pretty much everything that had happened since he'd come home, except meeting Joanna, had been a low point—he saw himself in love with her.

Even now, walking with his arm around her shoulder and hers around his waist as they went to see Kimimela, it felt like love. And this love certainly did not feel like anything he'd ever felt before. He knew lust, fondness and infatuation. But this was none of those. Meaning, in terms of his life, he couldn't define it. Or perhaps he was afraid to. It was all a big blur to him at the moment, and right now he had to concentrate on Kimimela and nothing, or no one else. He, not Joanna, was the one who would soon break her little heart into pieces.

"I've never had to do this,'' he said. "Telling a child her mother has died. How do you find the words?'' he asked as they stepped up onto the Chamberlains' wooden steps. "How do you tell someone that her life has just changed for ever?"

"With your heart, Chay. And with whatever else it was you found inside yourself to help Donna." She reached up and gave him a tender kiss on the cheek, than sat down in a faded white wicker chair on the porch. "You're the one she needs."

And Joanna was the one *he* needed.

Chay saw Kimimela's eager face at the window and braced himself for the hardest thing he'd ever had to do.

Joanna heard Chay's words, heard Kimi's muffled cries turn to sobs, and she bit her lip to hold back her own sobs. She knew the pain, knew the anguish that would follow for many years. Even now she sometimes cried for her own mother, and it was a deep hole in her soul that would never quite be put to rest. Right now she ached for both of them in there, Chay and Kimi, and there was so little she could do to ease their pain.

"Kimimela and I are going for a cherry cola," Chay said a little while later. Kimi was clinging to his left hand, still struggled against sobs. Chay held out his right hand for Joanna. "We need you to come with us."

A few minutes later, three dimes by the side of the cash register, the three of them sat in one of the booths near the front window. Kimi wasn't much interested in her drink. She went through the pretense of taking a few sips, but each time she did so her bottom lip gave way to a big tremble and the tears started flowing. And each time that happened she cuddled even harder into Chay. In some ways she was lucky having someone to cuddle into. When Joanna's mother had died, her father had cuddled into a bottle of whiskey and Joanna had been left to herself.

"DocChay said my mommy was a horse spirit," Kimi finally said. "That a horse spirit is very brave."

"And what else did I tell you?" Chay prompted.

"That she loved me very much."

"My own mother went away when I was your age," Joanna said. "But she didn't have a horse spirit to take her. I think your mother was glad to have a horse spirit."

"What kind of power animal did your mommy have?" Kimi asked.

"She didn't have one," Joanna said. "Where I came from people don't have power animals to help them like your mommy had."

"Do I have one?" Kimi asked.

Joanna looked at Chay. "I don't know much about those things, Kimi." Would he tell her? she wondered.

"DocChay calls me Little Butterfly. Is that my power animal?" Finally, a little farther away from the immediacy of her mother's death, Kimi began to relax. She even took a little more interest in her soda, Joanna was relieved to see. Of course, this was only the first hurdle for her. There were so many yet to come.

"You *are* a little butterfly," Chay said. "Which means you have great courage for the changes you will have to make. The butterfly will help you through these changes, help you to find the place you're meant to be."

"Is DocJo a butterfly, too?"

"No, DocJo is a hummingbird, I believe." He looked across the table at Joanna and smiled. "Someone who searches for the sweetness of life. A hummingbird's long tongue lets it bypass the often tough and bitter outer layers of a flower or plant to find the hidden treasures lying deep within. It's said that hummingbirds bring love as no other power animal can, and her presence means joy to everyone around her."

"That's lovely," Joanna whispered.

"That means we can both fly," Kimi squealed in delight. "Can you fly, too, DocChay? Are you a hummingbird or a butterfly like DocJo and I are?"

"He's a deer," Joanna said, her gaze fixed on Chay. She waited for a response from him, but all he did was pick up his cherry cola.

It was near suppertime when Joanna and Chay returned Kimimela to the Chamberlains' home. For a while her mother's death had been put aside, but now that the moment was over, Kimi clung to Chay with a fierceness Joanna had never seen in someone so young. She wasn't about to be left behind again.

"I'll come back to see you tomorrow," he promised.

"That's what my mommy said," Kimi screamed, holding on to him for dear life as Emil Chamberlain tried to lift her from Chay's arms. "Please, don't leave me, DocChay. Please. I want to go with you."

"Let me have her," Joanna said, trying to take Kimi into her arms. "Will you come with me, Kimi?"

Kimimela gave Chay the most forlorn look Joanna had ever seen, but didn't fight when Joanna took her. They went only to the wicker chair on the Chamberlains' front porch, where Joanna held and rocked Kimi for the next hour, whispering things to her that a grieving child needed to hear, things Joanna had needed to hear but never had. Then finally, when Kimi was exhausted and dozing off, Joanna took her to the Chamberlains' guest room, laid her down on the bed, and promised her she would be back. Kimi was long asleep by then, but even so, Joanna stayed there another twenty minutes before she went back to her own bed above the clinic and fell into it, into Chay's arms.

"What's going to happen to her?" she asked.

"Tribal law will keep her here, with her own. Someone will take her in. Maybe even the Chamberlains, since she' already there and their own children are already grown. Whatever happens, Kimimela will have a family here, one way or another.''

"It's so tough, though. She's scared right now, and nobody can understand the depth of that fear."

"You can," he murmured, pulling her close to him.

"You're good with her," Joanna said. Good, natural, caring. All the things Kimi would need in a father. Things *she'd* never had.

"I'm not keeping her," he said. "I know it seems like it might be a good thing right now, and she's a great kid, but Kimimela needs some stability. And that's not me. I live a bachelor's life in Chicago, a bachelor-without-kids life. Besides, she needs to stay here, with people who can teach her about her heritage. Look, I'll talk to my mother tomorrow and see if she has a suggestion. She probably would have taken Kimimela herself, except now with my dad…'' He dragged in a tired, ragged breath. "But she might know someone since Donna did work for her. It'll work out, Joanna. I promise you that. One way or another it will work out.''

Not always, Joanna thought. It hadn't for her. She didn't want Kimi going through what she had. First one family then another. People who'd only wanted her when it had been convenient. Kimi needed a better life, deserved a better life. And had it not been for the fact that she wasn't a Sioux, like Kimi, she might have taken the child herself. But that wouldn't be allowed because, as Chay had said, they would take care of their own. Kimi was their own. As much as Joanna felt at home here, she wasn't.

Snuggling into Chay, Joanna had a sudden vision—her, Chay, Kimi. A family. Nice, but not possible. It was a vision that would break her heart if she kept it. And she did so want to keep it. "Sometimes life just isn't fair," she murmured.

"But sometimes it is." He gave her a gentle kiss on the forehead. "Now, how about that nap...?"

"I need something else first," she said, tilting her face up to him for more than a gentle kiss on the cheek.

It was still dark when he awoke, and Joanna was still snuggled into him. They'd made love with amazing ferocity, despite their exhaustion, then she'd cuddled up to him and slept. And she hadn't moved all night. Spooning with him, with her naked body pressed into him—just feeling it there started his day off with a rousing dilemma he didn't need. He was scheduled to go home today, and back into his regular surgical rotation tomorrow. Hip replacement bright and early in the morning, and Mrs Wilmer had waited a good long time for it. Putting her off wouldn't be right. But with everything going on here, leaving right now wouldn't be right either. "Damn," he muttered, slipping out of bed.

He was headed downstairs to make a call to his partners, but he was still naked and there was no telling who might be lurking down there. It was a public clinic after all. People here respected privacy so no one would breach the stairs into Joanna's apartment, but that might not be the case elsewhere so, instead of dressing, which he intended to do after his shower, he went to the phone in the tiny kitchenette and dialed one of the partners in his practice.

"Look, Rob, it's really a mess here. My dad's still in critical condition, my mom's with him day and night. And my grandmother... Anyway, I'm not going to make it back tomorrow." Neither could he come close to promising a date. He listened to Rob Liebman complain for a few minutes, even though Rob was a good guy and a great surgeon. Rob would take care of things on that end, maybe even water his philodendron if he asked, although it was probably already dead. "I'm really socked in here, man. All kinds of obligations hitting me every which way and, to be honest with you, there's not going to be a graceful way of getting out of it.'' And there were long minutes now when he wasn't sure that he wanted to. Staying here with Joanna and Kimimela, taking care of his mother and grandmother... He felt the tug. But he also felt the overwhelming obligations, the ones he had turned his back on years ago.

So maybe he should be turning his back again. That was a thought not too far from the front of his mind. Standing there shoulder to shoulder with it, however, was this totally irrational notion that *he* might be the butterfly in transformation, that his was the change being made. ''Look, I'll get back to you in a couple of days and let you know my plans. Maybe I'll come home. God knows, what I have going on back there is a whole lot easier than what I have going on out here.''

He clicked off, then crawled back into bed with Joanna, pulling her against him once more. One more hour, he promised himself. One more hour, then he'd face the day. And the decisions.

Nestled into Chay's embrace, Joanna opened her eyes. She'd heard the phone conversation and of course he had to go home. That had been clear from the start. But knowing it hurt very much anyway.

CHAPTER ELEVEN

"HELICOPTER?" Chay asked. "You're going by helicopter?" They were on the outskirts of Rising Sun just after dawn, and the helicopter was sitting several hundred yards away from the Jeep, stirring up enough dust to obscure the remnants of a spectacular sunrise.

Joanna squinted into the sunrise anyway. Even when she couldn't see it, knowing it was there always gave her hope for the new day. "Believe me, if there was a better way, I'd take it. But I don't know what's going on up in Douay, and from the symptoms I've heard I don't have time to drive." She grabbed her medical bag and her duffel from the seat of her Jeep and looked wearily at the chopper. Definitely not her favorite mode of transportation by any means, but necessary at times. Especially right now. "Don't know when I'll be back either. This might take a few days." A few days if she was lucky. Many more if she wasn't. And maybe he'd be gone by the time she returned to Rising Sun, but that was her life. Little bits of disjointed pieces never quite fitting together to form anything whole or permanent. This morning's call from Douay had been about three members of the White Eagle family who were all sick. They shared the same symptoms, and those symptoms weren't good.

"Do you need some help up there?"

Such a nice thing to hear Chay offer, but the fewer people exposed the better, if this turned out to be what she thought it was. "No, I'll be fine." Besides, a few days' working with Chay had spoiled her, and now it was time to get unspoiled, and this was as good a way to do it as any.

136

"You're being pretty vague about this, Joanna, but I'm guessing you know what you're getting yourself into. Right?"

Yes, she certainly did know, in more ways than simply the medical. Right now, though, her job was the only thing that mattered because shortly she'd be seeing symptoms such as chest pain, fatigue, some weight loss, generalized chills and fever. All this had been spread out over a few weeks, according to Lawrence White Eagle. Of course, nobody had paid much attention because no one was really sick enough to stay in bed. Lawrence had mentioned to Joanna he thought it was a lingering cold or a simple case of flu.

Then last night his wife, Rachel, had started coughing up blood. She was the first in the family with that ominous symptom, but it had scared Lawrence enough to put in the call to Joanna first thing this morning, especially since his five-year-old daughter and his mother were showing some of the same symptoms.

"Mycobacterium tuberculosis maybe," Joanna said, trying not to sound too alarmed. The mere mention of TB always brought a hard chill down on the crowd, and while she'd never seen the disease on the reservation she always knew it was a possibility, especially among the Native American populations where the incidence was twice that of anybody else in North America. Unfortunately, several members of the White Eagle family were displaying the classic symptoms, which was why there had been no protest from her superiors over her request for a helicopter. Some conditions didn't merit a debate over costs, and for her bosses in Billings this was one of them.

"You're not serious, are you?" Chay asked, obviously trying to dredge up the disease that most physicians had relegated to dusty corners in their mental archives, since the general assumption was that it had disappeared years ago. "TB? Do you think you're really dealing with TB?"

"Yes, I think so. There are still about sixteen thousand cases of it reported in the United States every year. No particularly bad outbreaks, but in little clusters. And I think that's what this could be, judging from the symptoms I've heard. A little cluster." She hoped it was only a little cluster.

"Well, I'll be damned."

"My sentiments exactly when I found out." She glanced over at the chopper pilot who was waving her to the aircraft. "Look, Chay. I'm not good at goodbyes. I know you're going back to Chicago soon, and I may not be here when you leave. So thanks. Thanks for everything. It's been nice having another doctor around for a few days. It made the job less lonely." She leaned into the Jeep, gave him a quick kiss on the cheek, then turned and ran to the helicopter before she had a chance to think about what she'd just done. She'd given the man she could quite possibly love, maybe even for the rest of her life, a casual thank you, then the brush-off. But that's all she could do. Her reality wasn't his, and *this* was her reality.

As the chopper lifted her into the air and turned north, she didn't look down, couldn't look down to see him one last time. This job was all about broken hearts, and she'd just have to learn to get used to it. Or not put hers out there to be broken again.

On the ground, Chay watched Joanna disappear into the clouds. Then he headed to the nearest telephone.

Lawrence White Eagle was sick, too, as it turned out. Mild symptoms like everybody else, but they were developing and when Joanna arrived he was running a slight fever. His brother, Ernest, was symptomatic, too, Joanna discovered. Definite fever, a mild cough rattling around in his chest that he tried hard to stifle. But he clutched his chest when a spasm of coughing seized him then left the room, and Joanna wondered if he, like Rachel White Eagle, was experiencing hemoptysis—coughing up blood.

The entire clan lived in the same house with very little separation of living spaces. Seventeen of them, all from various generations, resided under the same roof, so to speak. It was more like a compound than an actual house. Several structures tacked together for the convenience of proximity. A nice, tight-knit family structure, but one Joanna feared could have serious consequences for those many of the White Eagles she'd yet to examine, because the spread of mycobacterium TB was through coughing and sneezing. People in close proximity to someone with TB risked breathing in the bacteria being sprayed out by someone infected, and becoming infected themselves. With so many people under the same roof, the possibility of an epidemic existed without any of the family members even breaching the confines of their own walls.

"OK," Joanna said to Lawrence, once she'd taken a quick assessment of the situation in his home, a veritable breeding ground for TB. "First thing I need for you to do is have everybody put on a mask." She handed him a box of disposables. "No exceptions. Plus hand washing. Lots of it." Those precautions probably came much too late, but they made her feel better. "And anybody who is obviously sick, such as you, needs to be separated from those who don't seem to be sick. In the meantime, I have to take a look at everybody who's not feeling well, even if it seems to be something minor like a headache, tiredness, fever, chills. Anything out of the ordinary. Also, I'll be testing everybody here once my supplies arrive, and giving the ones without the sickness a vaccination."

"I can pay," Lawrence said, his voice resolute, albeit muffled, from underneath the mask he was tying behind his head. "I can take care of my family." Over the months

Joanna had received more forms of payment than she'd known existed—sewing, mechanical work on her Jeep, food, livestock. While she didn't always know what to do with her bounty, nothing was ever turned down because paying was a matter of pride, even though the bulk of everything necessary for medical care came from Indian Medical Alliances without regard to anybody's ability to pay.

"Good, then we'll work out the details when I've finished here, if that's acceptable."

Lawrence smiled. "Thank you."

"So, let me go take a look at the rest of your family and see what's up." Then after that she needed to do the same with the rest of the one hundred and fifty residents of Douay. This was going to be a long couple of days, and in Douay there was no place for her to stay. No makeshift clinic, no front room like she used at Mrs Begay's. Nothing.

Indian Medical Alliances had testing supplies and medications on the way and her first order of business was to go scrounging for a place to store them, one where she could stay, too. Any little room away from the flow of TB spray would do nicely.

Outside, on the dirt road, Joanna took off her mask and gloves. Talk about isolated. This town was so far beyond the end of the road that the end of the road wasn't even visible from there. It was just a smattering of weathered, wooden houses dotting about a mile of barren countryside. The only thing that marked it as a town was the Douay welcome sign, plus the Douay garage and gas pump, owned by the White Eagle family, sitting across the street from their compound. The garage stocked a few dry good necessities on a couple of shelves inside, kept its gasoline pump full since there wasn't another pump around for miles, and was the place where the old-timers gathered on the wooden porch outside when they wanted to get away from home

Right now, two of them, typical Sioux elders with graying black braids streaming down to their waists, were seated out front on stools, with a wooden crate propped between them. She guessed there would be a checkerboard on the crate, because they were fixed on their game, whatever it was.

Over her months on Hawk, Joanna hadn't come to Douay too often. The folks here didn't have need of her, and when she did show up, no one ever came in for medical services of any kind. A very independent lot, she'd decided a long time ago. Half the men, like more than half the men spread throughout Hawk, lived and worked on the ranch, driving home on Friday nights to bring groceries and other supplies and be with their families and returning on Sundays. And they knew where she was when they needed her. Like today.

Yes, definitely isolated, she thought, looking up at the helicopter making its way to the little enclave.

It landed in the middle of the main road, which really wasn't a road so much as a wide spot between houses. Knowing the amount of dust it would kick up, Joanna dashed as far away from the landing spot as she could and turned her back to it, because any dust applied to her might well be permanent until she returned to civilization. She chuckled. Most people wouldn't even consider Rising Sun civilization, but compared to this it was a thriving metropolis.

"Joanna!"

His voice caught her by surprise. Spinning around, Joanna saw Chay hurrying toward her, carrying a large cardboard box. "What are you doing here?" she called over the whir of the chopper.

"Found a ride heading this direction so I thought I'd come along."

She was so glad to see him she wanted to throw herself into his arms, but they were otherwise occupied. "And you brought me a present?"

"Lots of PPD and tuberculin syringes." PPD, purified
protein derivative, was injected under the skin as a means
of diagnosing TB. At some point in the next couple of days
everyone in Douay would be tested. "Some BCG vaccine."
Bacille Calmette-Guerin vaccine used as a TB preventative.
"And a few other goodies." He set the box down and
headed back to the helicopter. The next box he hefted contained other basic medical supplies—IV setups, bags of normal saline. She hoped she didn't have to go that far in her
treatment. Then came the medicines—isoniazid, more commonly called INH, which was the most popular treatment.
Plus ethambutol to give along with the INH to help prevent
those who already had TB from spreading it any further and
streptomycin, an antibiotic helpful in treating secondary infections that might arise.

"You don't happen to have a pup tent and a couple of
cots with you, do you?" she asked after his third trip with
more supplies, the trip where he waved the helicopter a safe
trip back to Billings.

He winked. "I can do better than that, but it's going to
take a few hours."

"What?"

"The real present I'm bringing with me. So what's the
deal here? Have you had time to figure it out?"

"I've only had a look at the White Eagles, and there are
five cases for sure. Without testing, of course, but the symptoms are pretty advanced. And they're living in a house with
seventeen people so we could have a lot more people with
either the active or latent disease." Active meant it had de-
veloped into the full-blown sickness, latent meant the person
had been exposed to TB but, instead of it developing into
the illness, it was lying dormant in the body, without any
symptoms. With treatment, latent TB usually never devel-
oped into the disease. "And I don't have a clue about the

rest of Douay. Haven't even ventured out to take a look yet.''

"Is everybody you've seen so far stable?"

"The one who's really sick is Rachel, and I've got her cooling down with ice packs right now, plus drinking fluids. She's had a bout of hemoptysis, but not too bad, all things considered. Nothing that requires hospitalization for now. Just medication and rest.'' Good thing, because unless it was a life-or-death concern, she knew the White Eagles would submit themselves to no more than that.

"How the hell did they get TB out here?" Chay asked, picking up the first box to move it out of the middle of the roadway.

"Actually, they had a small outbreak of it in Fort Belknap a few years ago. It happens. Maybe someone from over there who's a latent made contact with someone here who's prone. Who knows?"

"And you've treated it before?"

"That's about all I treated when I was in Haiti. At our clinic we saw other patients, but TB was, and still is, endemic there.''

"So is this risky for you, being around the disease so much?"

"No more risky than it is for anybody else.'' She smiled at him and pulled a yellow surgical mask from her pocket. "I never leave home without one of these. Oh, and before you start mingling with anyone, you need to take the vaccine. And I'd prefer that instead of you coming into direct contact with people who have the diagnosis, especially in contained areas such as the White Eagle house, you stay in the open air. TB's not like it used to be, and it's pretty easily treated and controlled, but there's no sense taking unnecessary risks when you don't have to.''

"So what you're saying here is that you're the boss?" He grinned at her. "Like that night at Fishback Creek?"

"As I recall, you were the one who dragged me down there."

"As I recall, you were the one who insisted on getting naked up there on the butte." He pulled her into his arms. "And I've got to tell you, never having been naked on the butte before, it wasn't all that bad."

She loved the feel of his arms, and she was glad her goodbye a little while ago hadn't been a goodbye after all. Even a few extra minutes with Chay was worth the additional suffering she'd go through when he did leave. "I'm glad you came here," she said.

"Is it me you want here, Joanna," he asked, his voice suddenly so serious, "or is it the doctor you want?"

In answer, she snaked her hands around his neck and pressed her lips hard to his. It was a brief kiss, because in her life there was time for little else, but it was one full of her true answer, if only he could understand it. Within seconds it was over, and Joanna was the one to pull away. It was either that or lose herself in him, and that need was far outweighed by others.

"Look, I'm going back to finish examining the White Eagles and help with some kind of temporary setup to keep the sick ones isolated, then administer the skin tests. Maybe you could go door to door and ask if anyone has symptoms. Let them know that as soon as we can set up something sanitary we'll be doing skin tests on everybody. And I'll bet if you're nice, you can borrow Lawrence White Eagle's truck." Smiling, she pointed to the three-decades-old rusted Chevy leaning against the side of the White Eagle compound. "Not as nice as that BMW rental you've got back in Rising Sun, but it will get you there. I hope."

"Think I'll walk," he said, eyeing the bald front tires. "You know we're going to have to talk about this sooner or later, don't you? About us. Right now it's OK to hide behind all these medical crises and rusty trucks, but sooner or later it's going to have to be just the two of us. There will be a few minutes when we don't have to rush after a broken leg or a diabetic coma. When we don't have to squeeze everything into so little time. You avoided it when you left this morning, but I don't want to.''

"Why, Chay? So you can tell me that you're going back and I can tell you that I'm staying? What good's that going to do either of us? Your life is what it is, and mine's what I want. You work in a hospital, take care of people with insurance and nice cars. I work here and take care of people with nothing. I always have and I always will, and that's part of me that I can't change no matter what other kinds of feelings I might have going on…especially for you. So why complicate things? We've had a good time together, we even work well together. But that's all it is, Chay. That's all it can be, so why can't we just leave it alone instead of making it harder than it already is?''

He smiled patiently at her—a smile that should have mellowed her, but she couldn't afford mellow, not after working so hard on being detached about all this. Detached on the outside, anyway. "I'm sorry. I know we probably should have never started this, but—''

"Like I said,'' he interrupted, "sooner or later it's going to be the two of us without a medical crisis to pull us apart. It's going to happen, Joanna, and I swear to God I don't know what it is or how it will turn out. But it will happen, and avoiding it doesn't mean that what we've got going is solved or put away or quenched. Because it's not.'' He kissed her lightly on the forehead, turned and strode across the road to the first house on the other side.

"It won't work, Chay,'' Joanna whispered as she watched him knock on the door, put on his mask then go inside. "No matter how hard you try to figure it out, it won't work.'' Sighing for the things that never could be, Joanna ran back to the White Eagle house, praying her medical duties would overtake the tears that were so close to spilling over.

Her career and her personal life didn't mix and they never would. She'd learned that the first time with Paul. It was a lesson that should have stayed learned, and this time, with Chay, it would.

If she survived losing him.

It was early evening by the time Joanna and Chay met up again. She was exhausted, but glad to tell him that no more of the White Eagles had obvious symptoms. It would take a couple days for the results of the skin tests to appear, but in the meantime she'd started antibiotics and all the other TB-related drugs. The hardest part of the whole ordeal was getting the promise from Lawrence White Eagle that his family would continue the treatment after she was gone. Treatment would last for months, and naturally his concern was payment. So they'd struck a deal, and actually it was going to work out great for her. They would build a nice-sized addition to her clinic in Rising Sun, provided Macawi the rightful owner, approved it. Which she would. The White Eagle men were skilled carpenters, and their payment for the TB drugs would nearly double the size of the clinic. Now all she had to do was come up with the money for the materials.

That little chore would keep for another day. The White Eagles' payment for treatment was an open-ended contract they would honor whenever they were called upon to do so.

"So?" she asked Chay, resisting the urge to fall into his arms. That would have been the easiest thing to do, but she was desperately trying to toughen up. Sometimes she actually succeeded, like right now. Sure, it was only a small step away from him, but such a big one in so many ways.

"I have six with non-specific coughs, one with full-blown cold symptoms, no hemoptysis. And if you know anything about doing pelvics, Ruth DeLorme might be pregnant, or it might be menopause. She's not sure which, and I'm not doing *that* exam."

"How old is she?" Joanna asked, dropping down onto the stool next to the crate with the checkerboard.

"Mid to late forties, I'd guess. Didn't ask."

"Gosh, that's getting up there in age if she's pregnant."

Chay settled in across from her and moved a black checker diagonally. "You ever thought about having children?"

Joanna matched his move with a red checker. "Paul and I talked about it, but we didn't live the kind of life you'd want to bring a child into. Especially where we worked. Speaking of children, I called the Chamberlains a little while ago, and Kimi's doing as well as can be expected. Emil says she seems to understand the idea that her mother isn't coming back, and she doesn't even mention her. But she wants to know when you're coming to see her."

Chay made another move, then looked over at Joanna. "I can't do it. I guess that in a perfect world I'd adopt her and give her a happily-ever-after ending, but mine's not a perfect world and I can't raise a child in it."

"I think the Chamberlains are leaning toward adopting her. Emil says they're thinking about moving to South Dakota, to the Rosebud Reservation, to be closer to their family, and taking Kimi with them might work out."

"Uprooting her?" Chay shook his head adamantly. "She's already lost enough, and now they're thinking about taking away her home?"

"Giving her a home, Chay. And, believe me, I don't like it. But what else is there? She needs a family, the Chamberlains are a family." She slid her checker into another move. "I was actually thinking about keeping her myself. It wouldn't be easy, but I could make it work."

"So why don't you?"

"I'm not one of her kind, in case you haven't noticed. Not a drop of blood in me other than Irish, and that won't work."

"You'd be a great mom," he said, jumping her checker and grabbing it off the board.

"Well, I don't know about that, but I sure know when to cheat in a game to let the other person win, and that's definitely a mom skill."

He chuckled. "You expect me to cheat so you'll win?"

She double-jumped his checkers, then smiled. "Nope. It looks like I'll win without it. Care to have me beat you again?"

"You're bad, Joanna," he growled, resetting the checkers and gesturing for her to start the next game between them. "Of course, I kind of like being jumped by you. Maybe as much as you like being jumped by me. Admit it, you do like that, don't you?"

Joanna took a deep breath, then let it out slowly. Checkers as the metaphor. Such an implicit comparison. Suddenly she was so hot she needed a fan, or a block of ice to sit on. Or both. "One game at a time," she finally managed.

"One is a game, Joanna. The other is not." He jumped her checker and picked it up off the board, then leaned across the makeshift table and rubbed it lightly across her lips. "And when I win, I win for keeps."

"But you didn't win this one," she said, triple-jumping his latest move. Grabbing his checkers up off the board, she dropped them on her side, then stood up. "And you won't, as we seem to have company." Thank heavens! Because she was ready to take him right on the checkerboard, and it had nothing to do with those red and black game pieces.

Practically running for the road, Joanna watched a huge recreational vehicle roll into Douay. It wasn't quite the size of a full bus, but it would certainly sleep a good many people. A regular home on wheels. "Do you know someone in an RV?'' she asked, turning to see a mischievous glint in Chay's eyes—one that definitely wasn't the mischievous sexual glint she'd seen there only moments earlier. "Is this someone delivering that surprise you mentioned earlier?''

"It *is* the surprise," he said.

"What? You rented us an RV?''

"Nope. Bought it. Couldn't find a rental company who wanted to bring one out here in the middle of nowhere, so I bought it, offered the salesman a hefty little bonus to drive it out here himself, and now we've got a nice place to stay tonight. And to see our patients in the morning.''

"You're kidding?''

"Not kidding.''

"I've been saving up for the past three months to buy myself a new pair of boots and you just go and buy this...this...'' Joanna ran over to Chay, gave him a quick kiss on the lips, then ran to greet the salesman the second he stepped out the door. While he and Chay completed the sales transaction, then unhooked the car the salesman had towed in order to get himself back to Billings, Joanna explored the innards of Chay's rolling home. It had a separate bedroom, with a huge, king-sized bed. Had he ordered that specially? she wondered. *I'll take any old thing you have on the lot as long as it has a big bed?* Nice, fully equipped kitchen, cozy lounging area with several comfortable chairs, a dining room which she was already converting mentally into a place in which to administer the skin tests and vaccinations, an entertainment center with more equipment than she'd ever owned in her entire life, a bathroom to die for, including a luscious-looking shower. Oh, and a Jacuzzi. An honest to goodness Jacuzzi in an RV!

Truthfully, she'd never in her life lived in such a luxurious place, and by the time Chay wandered in to see if she liked it, she was waiting for him in the king-sized bed to show him just how much she did. Even if it was only for a day or two, it sure beat that cot in the back room of the garage that Lawrence White Eagle had offered her.

"I can't believe it," she said, rolling right into the middle and extending her arms to him. "This is absolutely the most wonderful RV I've ever seen. Actually, it's the only RV I've ever seen from the inside. So what are you going to do with it when you get it back to Chicago? Will there be room to drive it on the roads there?"

Chay pulled his dusty T-shirt off over his head. "Hell, I don't want it. Too big for my condo garage. It's yours. I figured when you go to some of the outlying areas, like Douay, it might be handy to take your own traveling clinic with you from time to time."

So much for all her resistance! "You know, Chay, somebody else might argue with you or tell you they don't want it, to take it back. But I want it. You don't know how much I want it and I'm not even going to try and pretend to be modest or humble here. Now that I've seen it, I don't think there's ever been anything I've wanted more in my life."

"I could take that the wrong way, you know."

She arched her eyebrows playfully. "I said *anything*, not *anybody*. Big difference, Doctor. Want to find out how much?"

"Want to find out how much I want to find out?" Chay tossed his hat on the dresser next to the bed and unbuttoned his jeans.

"Do you think the Jacuzzi works?"

"Salesman said everything's hooked up and fully functional."

"Are you hooked up and fully functional?" she asked. "Because I need to show you some appreciation like you've never seen before, and there's not a butte anywhere to be seen around here."

Resistance be damned. She'd try for it again tomorrow. Or the day after.

CHAPTER TWELVE

BY THE evening of Joanna's second day in Douay, everybody in town had been tested for TB and instructed on precautions, and now it would be another couple of days before positive results would pop up, if there were going to be any. Joanna was certainly keeping her fingers crossed on that one, because no one she had seen today had seemed symptomatic. Which was a good thing. Another good thing was that Rachel White Eagle was resting comfortably now, as were the other infected members of her family, meaning life was back to normal in Douay, and she could leave there for a little while instead of hanging around, taking care of them.

So for now she simply had to wait and see how the skin tests turned out. Of course, in *her* life there was no time to wait. Two of the White Eagle men worked on the ranch, which meant everybody there would have to be tested. By the time she arrived there tomorrow, the testing supplies would be waiting for her.

Well, so much for her day off. She'd actually planned to head back to Billings, buy that new pair of hiking boots, have the split ends of her hair trimmed, maybe go to a movie. A movie…how long had it been? Finding a place in the back row, eating that greasy popcorn she would tell her patients was so unhealthy for them, chasing down the popcorn with a box of candy and an extra-large soft drink full of sugar. So many of the goodies she couldn't, or wouldn't, eat anywhere near the reservation. But in the dark, maybe even with Chay, and she'd certainly intended to invite him into her little world of cinema decadence, two hours could have translated into a veritable vacation. And she was almost tasting it all, but unfortunately that taste was getting fainter and fainter by the minute. Maybe next week, or the week after.

Probably without Chay—a thought she didn't like thinking.

Joanna glanced wistfully out the side window of the RV. She was sitting in a comfy chair right now, feet tucked up, watching Chay chat with some old friends. He hadn't told her his plans yet. Last night in that wonderful king-sized bed she'd tried out some particularly fetching feminine wiles on him just to get him to open up to her, but he had some particularly fetching wiles of his own to use on her and conversation about anything had been the last thing on their minds. She sighed, thinking back to the king-sized bed. That was the way life was meant to be lived.

Then this morning it had been back to work as usual. All day, and so many people to see, people who hadn't known she and Chay would be there but wanted to be examined by a doctor anyway. Thank God the complaints had mostly been minor—aches, pains, nothing out of the ordinary. But like everything else, aches and pains took time, and at the time she'd expected to be on the road to the ranch, she'd been in the middle of explaining some typical osteoarthritis symptoms to Mapiya One Heart. She was somewhere over ninety, and very agitated that her knees had been giving her a few problems lately.

Joanna sighed. She couldn't even think ahead to her own life at forty, and Mrs One Heart was chattering away about the big party she was planning for her hundredth birthday in a few years, wondering if Will Two Crows would put her picture in the Hawk newspaper when the time came. Such long-range plans, Joanna thought. To be admired in Mapiya's case. In her own case, though, to be ignored.

Now, left alone to think, Joanna wondered about what was coming next. Leonard was stabilizing nicely, according to reports. At least he was out of Intensive Care now and had been transferred into a long-term, chronic care ward. Meaning there was nothing urgent about him any longer. Which was good.

So now all she had to worry about was diagnosing heaven only knew how many others like Leonard who'd neglected their health to a nearly fatal extent. Plus anybody with possible TB. And all that outside her regular duty of sore throats, menstrual cramps and an occasional wart.

"I need ten extra hours in the day," she moaned, getting up and heading forward to the driver's seat. As much as she wanted Chay to have these moments with friends, this behemoth certainly would not have the speed of her Jeep in getting on to her next medical chore, and she did need to get rolling pretty quickly in order to get it all done then get back here.

"OK, so it's a little large." Joanna climbed into the driver's seat, took a look at the steering-wheel and the foot pedals, then glanced over her shoulder at the total size of what she'd be driving. It was so long she couldn't see all the way to the back of it. "I can do this," she said, gritting her teeth. Thanks to Chay's generosity, for which she hoped to thank him another time or two before he left, this was her medical clinic on wheels now, and its purpose was fair compensation for its slowness. "No sweat. It's just like a car." She laughed. Yeah, right. No car could plow over buildings, trees, or other opposing structures the way this thing might if she wasn't careful.

"I take it you're driving?" Chay asked, climbing aboard.

"Got to learn some time. Now's as good as any."

"Want some help?"

"Nope."

"Coaching?"

"Nope."

He grinned at her. "Want me to run on ahead and post some warning signs that you're coming through?"

Joanna rose and snaked her arms around his neck. "The only warning signs I want posted are the ones that will tell me when you're coming through."

"Right now?" He tossed his hat over on the kitchen counter.

"Before we leave town?"

"Well, let's just say I was thinking about a nice, long shower before we head on back. I'm a little dusty…"

That was all he had to say. Joanna grabbed him around the waist and ground her hips into his. "It'll be a tight fit." She pulled her T-shirt over her head then tossed it, along with her baseball cap, on the kitchen counter next to Chay's hat. "That's better. Now we'll have lots more room."

Drawing in a ragged sigh, Joanna slipped into the warm shower spray and let the jets work their magic fingers over her for a little while as Chay struggled out of his dusty boots. A gentle steam rose up in the shower, fogging the glass door as she watched his distorted image through it. Even at so many blurred angles he was handsome—a handsome that went so much deeper than his surface. Sure, he probably went through his rotation of different women—men like Chay weren't meant to be alone. She thought about that, Chay and someone else. Thought about it, felt the jab in her heart like no other pain she'd felt in her life, then put it away because she was only spoiling what little time she had with him. And as much as she cared for him, even loved him, and she was afraid she did, she was pragmatic. She'd known what this relationship was going into it, and what it would be going out.

So for now the only thing to do was love the moment because their time was precious. Too precious to waste.

"Pardon me for asking, but we *were* going to spend some time in the shower together, weren't we?" Joanna laughed

"Because it's getting awful lonely in here all by myself, and if you don't hurry on in I might just have to...take a shower."

"Anything to oblige," he said, opening the door.

First glance revealed that he was ready. Very ready, she discovered as she pulled him into her arms. "You don't think everybody in Douay will think it's strange that we haven't left?"

He reached up and brushed a finger across her lips. "Don't think about anything right now," he murmured, tracing a path from her lips to her jawline. He lingered there for a moment, stroking her flesh so lightly she shivered against him.

Reaching up to his face, his beautiful face, she closed her eyes and ran her fingers over it as if to memorize every last detail. "Nice face," she purred, standing on her toes to brush her lips over his. "Soft skin. I like my men in soft skin."

Chay's hand slid down her belly, between her legs and she gasped. "And I like my women eager." He chuckled. "Are you eager?"

She placed a light kiss just below his ear, then nibbled his earlobe playfully. Then her tongue darted in and out of the hollow recess of his ear. "What do *you* think?" Sliding her hand down his belly, Joanna opened her eyes wide in astonishment when she found what she sought, and smiled boldly at him. "I do believe you're rather eager yourself," she teased, pushing her hips against the length of his hard shaft. She could feel his uneven breathing on her cheek and the uneven beating of her heart against his chest.

"Joanna," he murmured. *"Wakanda."*

"What does that mean?" she whispered.

"That you're a woman who possesses magical powers, and you do—over me." He caressed her neck, and she shuddered. Then he pulled her into his arms, and held her gently, exploring her shoulders with his lips. Her nipples were hard again, and as he rasped his tongue over them, they grew even harder. ''Joanna,'' he gasped again, pulling back. Everything was starting to happen too fast now. He wanted to enjoy her, to ravish every detail of their time together, to know every intimate inch of her and urge her to the same intimate exploration. More than anything else, though, he wanted to stretch this evening into an eternity. But the demands of sweet release were already threatening, and just as he ached for so much more than only the sexual release. So Chay moved back to the wall of the shower opposite her.

It was a brief stay, though, as he was driven to study and memorize her every detail. Joanna was so perfect, standing there waiting for him, her smile so tempting. So many possibilities, he thought, opening his arms to her and watching her fall into them and push herself once again to his full length. So many...

Brushing her breasts across his chest, she held her face up to him, pressing her mouth hungrily over his, and he could feel her pulse beat wildly against his chest, could feel the wetness of her tongue probe the depths of his mouth, seeking out all the recesses and delicate places. As she lifted her left leg and wrapped it around his right, and he took firm hold of her bottom and pulled her hard to him, he realized something in the passion of the moment that he'd been trying to fend off. He loved Joanna Killian. Dear God, he loved her. And he had to bite his lip to keep from shouting it out as they found their rhythm together. Mixed with the spray of the shower, the heat, and the raw emotions overtaking him, Chay shuddered to a climax that was far more soul-shattering than anything he'd ever thought could exist.

Afterward, as the shower spray was turning cool on his burning skin, he held her close and shut his eyes. Right there was a perfect moment, and he didn't want to ruin it with all the uncertainties.

*　　*　　*

Later, after they were on the road, while Joanna was driving and Chay was fixing a snack, Joanna finally got up the courage to ask him the question she'd been dreading. It had been on the tip of her tongue, even as they'd made love, but she hadn't wanted to spoil that moment. Even now, as she braced herself, she felt a queasiness in the pit of her stomach. But it had to be asked. There was no getting around it any longer.

"When are you going back to Chicago, Chay?" she asked, trying hard to sound casual about it. It was a long ride to the ranch, and there was plenty of time to do the asking. But there was no reason to wait any longer. She wanted to know when she needed to schedule a broken heart into her busy work days.

"Day after tomorrow. We'll test the workers at the ranch, then I'll go into Billings to see my mother and Macawi, and catch a plane back home."

Back home. His words seemed so matter-of-fact. Not cold, but not full of concern either.

So much for that phase of her life. That was that.

Early October

"I just need a quick dose of Compazine, that's all." Instead of disrobing as Greg Reynolds had instructed her to do, probably more for his own satisfaction than medical reasons, Joanna paced back and forth in the tiny cubicle in the emergency department. She wasn't a patient: she was there checking in on Leonard Ducheneaux, who was scheduled to be moved home in a day or two. But that stupid flu that had been following her around these past couple of days was playing fast and loose with her stomach. Compazine would quell the nausea, simple as that. Ibuprofen would take care of the headache. And a good night's sleep would work miracles for her. By morning she'd be good as new and ready to go back to Rising Sun.

"But I should examine you first," Greg said, grinning.

You wish, she thought. He wasn't bad company, Joanna decided. The couple of times they'd had dinner together and seen a movie had been nice enough. Somewhat pleasant. Definitely no expectations on her part, though, because she didn't do that any more. The only expectation in her life was for tomorrow's work.

"So how's the TB epidemic going out there?" he asked, finally handing her the paper cup with the pill.

"No epidemic. No one else tested positive, and everybody has been vaccinated. I'm still doing periodic checks, but so far we're OK." She popped the pill into her mouth and took the cup of water he offered. "I think we got lucky. Five positives and a couple of latent cases I'll be keeping an eye on, but that's it. And everybody who has it is back on their feet, doing well." She'd been lucky. Considering what she'd worked with in Haiti, very lucky.

"Well, Jo, epidemic or not, you're looking awfully tired."

"Hard work will do that to you." These days she was tired and then some, and the Indian Medical Alliances had told her she was mandated to take a week off as soon as they could find a temporary to replace her. As far as she was concerned, that couldn't be soon enough. On good days she considered going to see Chay during that vacation. They talked several times a week, but he'd never invited her, even after she'd mentioned taking some time off. So on her bad days she thought about sleeping for that whole week. Sleeping, eating, sleeping some more. And if this flu didn't let up, puking her guts out every now and then.

"Is that Indian doctor dude coming back to help you any time soon?"

"That Indian doctor dude has a surgical practice i

Chicago.'' She grimaced as another wave of nausea assaulted her, and grabbed the blue plastic basin Greg was holding out for her in case the nausea erupted.

''I'm sensing that tonight wouldn't be a good night to ask you out for pizza.''

Joanna rolled her eyes at him then vomited into the basin.

''How are you feeling, Leonard?''

He nodded politely. Physically, he was coming along. Some weakness on the left side compromised his arm and made him dependent on a quad cane, but he was walking now, several steps at a time. Only he wasn't talking. Hadn't said a word to anyone. The speech therapist had diagnosed him as aphasic, but Joanna wondered. Aphasia was an impairment of the ability to use or comprehend words, usually acquired as a result of a stroke or other brain injury. But when she looked into Leonard's eyes, she didn't see impairment at all. She saw the keen intellect she'd always seen there, making her think that this could be his stubbornness coming through—some form of protest rather than a malady.

''I've made arrangements to have you transferred home, and Wenona and Macawi will be taking over your therapy. You do understand that even though I'm letting you leave the hospital, you've got to continue working. You're not going to improve your physical function if you don't.''

He nodded again, then turned his attention to the window. His view outside was only the asphalt parking lot, and he stared at that parking lot for hours on end, she'd been told. Possibly depression. It happened. But she'd done everything she could to assure him that his outlook was good, because it was, if he was willing to do the hard work.

''I talked to Chay yesterday.'' She waited for a reaction, but, like every time she mentioned Chay's name, she never got one. "He's doing fine. He was promoted to the head of his department a couple of weeks ago."

Still no reaction. Heavens, this was a stubborn man. "He's the youngest person ever to make department head in orthopedics. I should think you'd be proud of him." She was proud of him, even if Leonard wasn't. "You're never going to forgive him, are you? He's made a success of his life, doing what makes him happy, but that's not good enough for you. And frankly, Leonard, I don't understand that. You've been glad to accept all the medical treatment we've been giving you, and you're smart enough to see how well you've done with it. In spite of it all, you're still shutting him out.

"Well, it hurts him, Leonard. But it hurts you, too. Healing has as much to do with emotional ailments as it does spiritual or physical, and all I can tell you is that Chay fulfils the role of shaman much better than you do, even though he's not convinced he believes in it. I actually saw him act as a shaman, and he was kind and generous and caring. And he cared for the whole person, not just parts of it. But I don't think you can do that any more, you've become so closed-minded. Sure, your extraction might have made our treatment of Michael Red Elk easier, but I'm not sure you could have sat with Donna Rousseau the night she died and guided her over the way Chay did. Which is what you're supposed to be about, Leonard. But you're not. You're the one who needs the extraction. You need to have your bad energy removed."

Even that didn't get a rise out of him, and she'd thought it would. Normally, she didn't react quite so forcefully with her patients, but she'd hoped a little force might push Leonard back in the right direction. She'd even warned Wenona about what she intended to do. But she'd failed. Leonard hadn't blinked, hadn't flinched, hadn't even expe rienced a change in breathing. Joanna headed to the door, drained.

At least the Compazine was kicking in. Maybe that was the best she could hope for.

"Will my son care for his child?" Leonard asked just as Joanna stepped into the hall. "Assume the responsibility of being a father like a man should do?"

Joanna spun back around. "His child?" she sputtered. Chay had never said anything about having a child. Not when they were together intimately, and not in the weeks since. She couldn't even comprehend the fact that Chay had a child somewhere. Certainly, he'd been good with Kimimela…

Oh, no! Not possible. But… Joanna did the math. Kimi was seven, Chay hadn't been there for eight years. Kimi had no known father. Chay had a particular affection for the little girl and, more than that, Kimi had such a strong bond to Chay the first time they met. Definitely possible!

The list was adding up too quickly, and she brought a mental halt to it. It was Chay's life, and there was nothing between them that had ever hinted at something permanent. So it was none of her business. None of her business that Kimi wasn't working out with any of the temporary placements set up for her, that she was sullen and unhappy and becoming a discipline problem. None of her business that Kimi might have a father who was more than able to look after her, but who refused. None of her business that Kimi adored Chay but, like Chay's own father, he had turned his back on his child. That was, if Kimi belonged to Chay.

No, this was none of her business at all. Even so, Joanna's stomach started to roil and she was forced to dart into Leonard's bathroom to vomit one more time. So much for the Compazine.

*   *   *

Settling into her Billings apartment for the evening, on medical call to no one for any reason for the next few hours, Joanna looked at the canned tomato soup she'd heated up for her supper, decided it was too bland to waste good effort eating it, and dumped it in the sink. Sleep was a better use of her time anyway, and since the nausea had finally died down and her head wasn't thumping, she took advantage and tumbled into bed well before eight o'clock. That would give her ten blessed hours before she had to return to Rising Sun. And hours asleep meant hours she didn't have to think about Chay.

It seemed like she'd been sleeping for ever when a knock at the door awoke her. Turning over to look at her clock, Joanna discovered it was only ten. Only two lousy hours of sleep and now someone was intruding on the rest she had coming to her.

Slipping into her bunny slippers, the blue pair she kept there, Joanna plodded to the front door, ready to give someone a good piece of her mind, and peeked through the peephole. It took several seconds for that face to register as she didn't expect to find *him* standing there. Once she did realize it was Chay, she opened the door.

He was grinning.

She wasn't.

"Did I catch you in the middle of something?" he asked, stepping in, dropping his overnight bag on the floor just inside the door.

"Other than a good night's sleep, no." She wasn't ready for this. Didn't want to face him, didn't want to ask him the question that needed to be asked. Didn't even want to resume what she was sure he'd assume they would resume now they were together again. "You didn't tell me you were coming." Not that it mattered any more.

"I wasn't sure until I found someone to take call for me for the next three or four days."

"Three or four days?"

He nodded. "That's all I have right now. My mother called and asked if I could get some things arranged at the house for her for when my father goes home."

"So you've come home to help your mother." Even to her ears, her words were flat, unenthusiastic. No, she didn't begrudge Wenona her time with Chay, but over these past six weeks, when Joanna had asked him if he was coming home, he'd put her off. *Get over it, Joanna. You're not enough of a draw to get him here. That's the fact, now let it go.* It had just been sex, and that was all she was to him.

It was finally beginning to sink in. *Hard.* "Look, I've got to go back to Rising Sun early. My bed's not big, so you can take the couch."

Chay pulled Joanna into his arms, placed a soft kiss on her lips and in spite of her best efforts to shrug it off, she shivered anyway. Shivered from the top of her head to the tips of her toes. *Damn it, anyway!* Why did he still have that kind of an effect on her even after she knew what she meant to him? Even when she tried so hard to fight it? "Or you can have the bed and I'll take the couch."

"A bed for one can be fun for cuddling," he said.

"Except when one of the cuddlers has flu." She pulled out of his arms. "I really need some sleep, Chay. We'll talk in the morning." Even though there would be nothing to say.

"Can I fix you anything?" His voice was so full of sympathy her heart started to break all over again. She'd only just started getting through the days without so much pain, and suddenly it was all coming back—the empty feeling, that sense of a vague hopelessness that nothing would ever be quite right in her life again. Just these last few days she'd been able to go for brief periods of time without thinking about him. But now...

Joanna shook her head as she and her bunnies shuffled back to the bedroom. Behind her closed door, she kicked off her bunnies, slid to the floor, and wept.

CHAPTER THIRTEEN

"LOOKS good," Chay said to Lawrence White Eagle, who was heading the reconstruction effort at the Ducheneaux home. Front steps gone, a ramp had been built instead. Handrails in the bathroom. A shower stall instead of a tub. All for a father who wouldn't acknowledge him, but Chay didn't bother with that. This would make his mother's life easier, and hiring the White Eagle men to make the renovations was the least he could do for her. If he could have hired a private nurse, he would have done that, too, but there were none available in that part of Montana. None who wanted to come to the emptiness of the Big Open.

"We'll go into Billings and get that lift chair for Leonard this afternoon," Lawrence said, "and that should just about do it. When he gets home, though, if there are any other changes he needs, just let me know and we'll take care of it."

"Would you mind making his office at the ranch accessible when you have the time?" Chay didn't know for sure if his dad would be able to return to work, but if there was any way Leonard could manage, Chay figured he would. "Same kind of changes you've made here. Ramps instead of steps, grab bars, whatever else you think is necessary."

"You're a good son," Lawrence said.

"Yeah, real good," Chay muttered, glancing across the front porch at Joanna, who was trying to calm down both Wenona and Macawi. They'd both wanted to ride from Billings to Rising Sun with Leonard, but the private hire ambulance company wouldn't allow it. So both women had spent the morning fretting and fussing, and now that the ambulance was fifteen minutes overdue they were nearly inconsolable, and the last thing anybody needed in the middle of all that were the bad feelings between him and his father. It would be a better transition for his dad, not having him there.

"Look, I'm going back to Macawi's now," he called to them. Instead of staying with Joanna, he'd been sleeping on his grandmother's couch these past couple of nights. No explanation other than Joanna was still recuperating from her bout of flu. Admittedly, he was disappointed. He'd hoped this trip would have turned out differently for the two of them, but she'd been pretty distant. In fact, if he hadn't known better, he might have thought she was trying to avoid him.

Hell, maybe she was. Certainly, over the weeks he hadn't given her any indication that their situation was other than it was—long distance. "Damn," he muttered, heading to his rental car. A father who snubbed him, now the woman he loved who avoided him. Could he make an even bigger mess of things?

"Will you wait?" Joanna called. "We might need you to help get your dad settled in."

Before he had a chance to answer, Chay saw the dust cloud kicking up down the road and knew that somewhere within it was an ambulance bringing his father home. Sure, he'd stay and take whatever his father handed him today. He was used to it.

Several minutes later Leonard Ducheneaux emerged from the ambulance, and with help from Wenona on one side of him and Joanna on the other walked up the ramp, right on by Chay without saying a word, and on into his house. Then he sat himself down in the same recliner in which he'd sat for the last twenty years, put his feet up and asked to see the latest edition of Will Two Crows' newspaper. It was like he'd never been sick, never left his home. This was simply another day in the life of Leonard Ducheneaux.

Another stubborn day like all the rest. Some things never changed, Chay thought as he handed the paper to his father.

"Thank you, Chayton," Leonard said.

Chay blinked in surprise, staring down at his father, who simply opened the paper, picked up his reading glasses from the table next to his chair, and began to read. "You're welcome, Dad," he replied.

He was wrong. Some things did change, and as he looked over at Joanna brushing her tears away with the back of her hand he smiled. Change was better than he'd ever expected it to be. And for the first time in eighteen years he knew he desperately needed it in his life—that change to permanence he'd never wanted before.

"I had them put extra pepperoni on it," Chay said, sliding the plate with an extra-large piece of pizza on it across the table to Joanna.

She slid it back at him. Her stomach was fine now, but the last thing she needed was something to upset it again. Tomorrow, first thing in the morning, she was off to Steele to take a look at Michael Red Elk's progress. He was coming along nicely, following all the rules she'd laid out and exercising. Then she had to drop in on Billy Begay in Flatrock to see how he was doing, managing his diabetes. It was tough going for a kid, but overall he was handling it pretty well. Much better than his dad, actually. So maybe the kid could be a good example for his father. Joanna could only hope.

"Sorry, but no pizza for me," she said, sliding back her chair and preparing to stand. "I'm still eating bland." Chay was going home tomorrow. He'd already mentioned that, so there was no wondering about it this time. And in a way she was grateful for the flu, because she'd been able to keep him at an arm's length because of it. "Look, I need to get up early—"

"I don't blame you," he interrupted.

"For what?"

"For avoiding me. But you've got to know, Joanna, that this isn't easy for me either. Coming home, seeing you…"

"Look, we had fun. We worked well together, we played well together. I knew from the start what it was, and I'm not complaining. And I wanted it as much as you did, Chay, so—"

"I love you," he said. "And damn it, Joanna, it's been killing me, being separated from you."

This was the moment she should have flown into his arms and confessed her love for him, too. But hearing the words she'd wanted to hear from him for so long hurt more than anything ever had before. Even more than the morning they'd made love for the last time and he'd said goodbye. She thought about their separate lives for a moment, and about Kimi, who desperately needed something other than separation. Maybe Chay turning his back on Kimi was what hurt Joanna the most, because she'd truly believed for a while that Chay was everything she wanted. But he couldn't be, not if he didn't honor his obligations. And while she might not be numbered among those obligations, Kimi certainly was.

"I love you, too, Chay," she admitted, almost sadly. Because she did, with all her heart. "But that's not enough."

Standing, she spun around to retreat to the sanctity of her curtained-off bedroom and nearly fell she was so light-headed. "Oh, my," she said, grabbing hold of the corner of the kitchenette table. "Maybe I should have eaten some pizza after all." Suddenly Joanna's knees started to buckle under her and she pitched forward, but before she hit the floor Chay jumped up from his chair, scooped her up into his arms and whisked her to the bed. "I really need a day off," she said, leaning her head against his chest.

The last thing she heard was the steady, comforting beat of his heart.

"Her blood pressure's a little low, but other than that her vital signs are fine." Chay tossed his stethoscope over on the table next to the bed and took hold of Joanna's wrist to check her pulse for the tenth time in an hour. Normal, as always. "She's dehydrated, and I'm guessing she hasn't eaten much for a few days."

Macawi patted him on the shoulder as she scurried into the kitchenette. "She's overworked. Maybe you should take her away someplace nice for a vacation."

"She gave me the brush-off just before she fainted." He flinched, thinking about it. Hearing that she loved him, then hearing that it wasn't enough. He would have asked her why but she'd chosen that particular moment to black out. Now, almost an hour later, she was intermittently sleeping, occasionally waking, but mostly sleeping. "And, believe me, if I thought Joanna would go, I'd take her."

Macawi put the kettle of water on to boil for hot tea, then spun around to her grandson. "So why wouldn't she go with you? What did you do to her?"

"You're blaming this on me?"

"Someone needs to take the blame. You love the girl, she loves you. The rest of it shouldn't be so difficult."

"Except that she won't come to Chicago. Which makes it real damn difficult."

A sly grin crossed over Macawi's face, followed by that devilish glint in her eyes. Chay knew he was about to get everything she had, and he had a hunch what it was going to be—something he'd been considering almost since the moment he'd left here weeks ago. "OK, beautiful, let me have it."

"It's simple. You stay." She took two tea bags out of Joanna's tin and dropped them into two mugs. "She stays, you love her, so you stay, too. That way she won't be passing out from exhaustion because there'll be someone here to help her."

Chay pulled a squeeze bottle of generic honey out of Joanna's cabinet and handed it to his grandmother. He couldn't remember how many times they'd had these serious talks over hot tea with honey. And he couldn't remember the last time they'd had one. "I've been thinking about it."

"And thinking gets you where, Chayton? Sometimes it's good to act with your heart, not your head."

He glanced over at Joanna, who was thrashing around in the bed. Such a restless sleep when she needed peace. "Believe me, I have been thinking with my heart. I'm worried about her, Macawi," he said, taking the cup of tea his grandmother handed him.

"And you should be, a woman all alone such as she is. You have a choice to make now, Chayton, and this time it has to be the final choice. No going back once it's done. You owe Joanna that much."

He owed Joanna that much. Truer words had never been spoken.

An hour later, sitting on the front step of the clinic, looking up and down the deserted road running though Rising Sun, he wondered if he could make it here. He wasn't the kid who'd never seen the world now. Wasn't the kid with no expectations other than where to get his next dime for his next cherry cola. He'd gone a long way away from here, and it was going to be a long way getting back. "Joanna," he murmured. And a long, miserable life without her if he didn't come back.

But even with Joanna, could he make it?

He sure as hell wanted to. He wanted to come back to

Rising Sun much more than he'd wanted to leave. But it
scared him. So many dreams had come full circle, leading
him right back to the beginning. It scared him, but leaving
here again scared him even more because, as much as he
questioned his ability to make it here, he knew he couldn't
make it anywhere without Joanna.

Sighing, Chay watched the lights from a single vehicle
make their way slowly up the road. "Turn around," he said
quietly. "There's nothing here for you." But the vehicle
kept coming anyway, persistent devil that it was. Someone
had a mission that wasn't to be thwarted. Like Joanna.

Joanna…God, he loved her. And even though she was
just upstairs, he missed her like crazy.

The intrepid vehicle stopped in the roadway across from
Chay, and it wasn't until he heard the familiar rusty creak
of its door that he looked up and saw his mother climb out.
"Come to commiserate?" he called, standing to greet her,
shocked to see that his mother had been the one driving.

"I came to bring your father."

"My…"

"He said he wanted to see you. That he *had* to see you."
Wenona scooted around to the passenger's door and opened
it. By the time Leonard had dropped both feet onto the
ground, Chay was there, holding on to his arm for support

"Why?" Chay asked.

Leonard didn't answer. Instead, he headed into Joanna's
clinic, leaving Chay with no other choice but to help him
across the road and inside.

Once there, Leonard sat down in the waiting room, then
went dead quiet.

"Did he tell you what this is about?" Chay whispered to
his mother.

"He told me that he had to come here. That I was to
drive him."

"But you can't drive. Why didn't you call me?"

"I can drive, Chay. I've always been able to drive. I've just never had a reason until tonight."

He chuckled. Joanna had been right. It was all about choices. His mother's choice, Joanna's choice, and now his choice. And, like his mother's, his choice did have a reason. "And you didn't ask him why he wanted to come?"

Wenona shook her head. "I'm going to go sit with Joanna for a while. You stay here with your father."

Wenona was barely up the stairs when Leonard looked up at Chay. "She bears you a child," he said. "With great difficulty."

"Who…? What?"

"Dr Killian bears you a son. But she needs help other than that which your medicine can give her."

Chay shook his head, unable to get past the first part of his father's pronouncement. "What do you mean, Joanna bears me a child?"

"You're the doctor, Chayton. Figure it out."

"When did she tell you?"

"She didn't."

"So you're what? Guessing?"

"Not guessing. I don't have to guess. I know."

"Oh, that's right. You're the shaman. You know these things."

"You're the shaman. If you were to look deep enough inside, you would know the things you need to know."

"So why didn't she tell me? She's been saying it's flu."

Leonard let out a deep sigh. "Because she believes it to be flu. It will be for you to tell her otherwise. Now, please, tell your mother to take me home."

Chay headed to the stairs, too numb to even comprehend the fact that his father knew Joanna was pregnant when Joanna didn't know that herself. "You said something about help that my medicine can't give her. I don't understand. What's that supposed to mean?"

"She suffers a deep brooding." Leonard didn't explain, didn't say another word. But after he was gone, and as Chay watched Joanna toss and turn in bed, he understood. Besides her exhaustion, Joanna was in emotional turmoil. She called his name over and over in her turbulent sleep, then rebuked him as he took her hand to comfort her.

"Joanna, what have I done to you?" he asked, trying to get a little orange juice down her the next morning.

"I'm just so tired," she said, shoving it away. "A little more sleep and I'll be fine."

"You need to eat, Joanna," he said.

"Tomorrow, promise."

She dozed off again, and this time her sleep was a little more restful. At least restful enough to give Chay a few minutes for a quick shower and a shave. In the bathroom, he looked at his face in the mirror while he combed his hair. "A son," he said. "*My* son."

He hadn't thought about it since his dad had dropped that bomb. It was too absurd to think that he would know when Joanna didn't. But as Chay studied the face in the mirror he saw something far deeper than his reflection. He saw the next generation. "Joanna," he whispered, gripping the edges of the sink to steady himself.

Her head hurt, and the light coming in through the slatted blinds was killing her. Rolling over, Joanna glanced at the clock. It was almost noon. Noon? The last thing she remembered was pizza…

She looked around for Chay, but he wasn't there. She could hear the water running in the shower, though. "Chay?" she called, sitting up.

Immediately, her head started spinning. "Whoa," she said, flopping back down onto her pillows. The instant her head hit them her stomach kicked in with a giant roll of nausea, and she turned over on her side to vomit. Only sh didn't vomit as she'd expected. She merely fell out of bed on the side opposite the bathroom door and landed in a heap on the floor between the bed and the wall. Too tired to crawl back up into bed, Joanna curled up on the throw rug there and went back to sleep, thinking that the next time she opened her eyes she'd feel better.

"Joanna?" Chay called as he stepped out of the bathroom. The bed was empty. He took a quick glance of the entire area, didn't see her, and called again. "Joanna?"

No answer. Had she gone downstairs? He ran down, took a look and didn't find her. Not in the examining rooms, not in her office, not even in the supply room. She simply wasn't there, so he headed outside to the RV, but she wasn't there either. "Where the hell are you?" he asked, heading over to his mother's diner to look through the window. Next he went to Macawi's, and like every place else Joanna hadn't been there.

"I don't have a clue," he told his grandmother. "I was in the bathroom for five minutes. She was in bed, then she wasn't." Macawi followed him back to the clinic and upstairs. Somehow he expected to find Joanna sitting at the little kitchenette table next to the window, laughing at him for being so silly. But she wasn't there. "She's pregnant," he told Macawi. "With my baby. Dad knew it and he told me I would also, if I wanted to."

"And you wanted to?" Macawi asked.

Chay nodded. "My baby, Macawi. *Our* baby. And I don't think she even knows it yet. She thinks she has flu."

"Are you going to marry her?"

"Hell, I've got to find her first."

Joanna heard the muffled voices. Chay's she recognized for sure. Macawi's she wouldn't have, except that Chay addressed her by name. Who were they talking about? Somebody pregnant.

Joanna rolled over and looked up at the ceiling. Somebody was going to have a baby? Several women on the reservation were pregnant right now—at least nine of them. And Chay had said it was *his* baby. "Our baby," she mouthed, reaching down to feel her belly.

No! How could that be? She wasn't pregnant. Surely she'd know the difference between flu and that. Wouldn' she?

Hands still on her belly, Joanna shut her eyes and tried to think. Sure, she'd missed her last menstrual period, bu she was under so much stress she hadn't thought anything of it. And she was on the Pill. Had she skipped any days No, of course not.

Rubbing her hands over her belly, she wondered if Chay was talking about someone else. First there had been Donna so maybe there were others, too. Why not? She'd known al along that men like Chay had others. She might live in an isolated area, but she wasn't dumb about these things. That had to be it. Probably somebody back in Chicago—the reason he didn't want her coming there. And telling her he loved her had just been the line he used. It meant nothing

Stupid her. She'd told him she loved him, and it mean everything. How many other women had fallen into the same trap? she wondered. The same foolish trap.

Joanna raised her head off the rug and looked down a her flat belly. For a moment, when she'd thought maybe sh was carrying Chay's child, the feelings shooting through he had been like nothing she'd ever known in her life. But wasn't so, and suddenly she felt sad and empty.

"Joanna?" Chay bent down, picked her up and put her bac in bed. "I'm so sorry. I didn't know you were down ther

I've been looking everywhere for you. Are you all right? Did you hurt yourself?''

"Fine," she said. "I'll be better in a little while after I've had more sleep."

"I think I need to take you to the hospital," he said. "You're dehydrated, weak…"

"I'm fine. And I'm not going to the hospital." She rolled over and turned her back to him. "Just go away and leave me alone. Lock up downstairs on your way out so nobody else comes in."

"I'm not leaving," Chay said.

"Yes, you are."

Chay ran his fingers through his hair, wondering if he should tell her now or wait until she was feeling better. He didn't know how she would take the news, didn't even know if she wanted children right now with the way she was devoted to her work…even though she'd considered taking Kimimela in. But Kimimela wasn't a baby.

Joanna would be a good mother, though. A great mother. He couldn't think of anyone better to be the mother of his child. Maybe if she knew she'd eat a little, for the baby's sake. Or take some fluids. She was weak, and so dangerously close to needing medical help that if she didn't eat or drink something soon, he would have to take her to Billings, whether or not she wanted to go. He didn't want to do anything against Joanna's wishes, even if it was for her own good, but he might not have a choice.

He kissed the back of her hand and held it, then shut his eyes. *She suffers a deep brooding.* His father's words.

Deep brooding and dark thoughts, taking up her good energy, energy she needed for their baby. The words were from his heart, deep within him, and he knew what he had to do. For her, and for their child—his and Joanna's.

Maybe he'd known it for hours, or for ever, but now he

could put it off no longer. Scooping her up in his arms, he carried her down the stairs and out to her Jeep.

"I don't know if you can hear me, Joanna, or if you want to hear me, but I'm going to make this better for you. I promise, it's going to get better. Everything will. Very soon."

CHAPTER FOURTEEN

THE trip to Fishback Creek took much longer than Chay would have liked, but he forced himself to drive slowly for Joanna's sake. Wrapped in a blanket and curled up in the seat, she barely stirred over the three hours, and he hardly thought about anything else except what he was about to do.

A trip to the hospital might have been the wisest thing, and maybe that was where the journey would end anyway. But he was reacting to something much deeper surfacing in him, something that he'd tried to block out for most of his life. He was a shaman as well as a doctor. He possessed the gifts and training, as his father and the generations before him had. As his son might one day.

Certainly he trusted his medical judgment much more than anything else, and his medical judgement leaned toward getting Joanna to Billings, starting an IV, convincing her to eat something. That would get her back on her feet and once there she would do the right thing by their child. He was sure of that.

But every time he closed his eyes he saw the dark energy enveloping her. It was like a dense cloud hanging so low she couldn't find her way out of it. What was worse, she wasn't trying.

Deep brooding. That wasn't a medical problem, at least not yet.

Nearing Fishback Creek, Chay cut off the road and headed toward the butte. Their butte. Against the backlight of the moon, he could see it ahead. Perfect and quiet. The place where Joanna needed to be.

And the place where he needed to help her in the only way he knew how.

"Evening moon, evening moon, come my way, come my way. Take her pain, take her pain. Down below, down below. To healing waters down below, down below."

Through her bleariness, Joanna heard the gentle night song. It repeated itself through her haze over and over, and each time she wanted to wake up to it. But she couldn't, not yet. It was like awakening would stop it, and she didn't want it to stop. Somehow it reassured her, comforted her. So she listened for a while as the quiet chant continued. When she finally did open her eyes it was morning, and as if by magic she felt better. Not tired. Flu all gone.

Where was she? She looked around, expecting to find herself in bed, but she was out in the open. She knew this place—the butte. Their butte. But how had she got here?

"Chay?" she called, suddenly alarmed.

"Down here," he called back from the creek.

Shoving off her blanket, Joanna stood up, still not sure what was going on. She didn't remember coming here. The last thing she remembered was refusing pizza from him. Then there had been some strange dreams... She'd thought she was pregnant, but it was flu. One thing she remembered for sure was that Greg Reynolds had given her Compazine to cure the nausea going along with her flu. But that had been when? She couldn't remember.

Chay wandered back up from the creek carrying a small stone bowl full of water. "How are you feeling?" he asked.

"Fine. Nausea's gone. And I'm not tired. But I don't have a clue what we're doing up here."

Pouring the water on the ground, now that the extraction was complete, Chay set the bowl aside. "It's a long story."

"Was I doing peyote or something? Is that why everything's such a blur?"

He laughed. "No. And I'm not really sure how to explain it."

"Try," she said, grabbing up the blanket. "On the way back to Rising Sun. I've got patients to see, especially since I've had a little time off." She turned and headed to the edge of the butte, then glanced back to see if Chay was following, only to find him sitting atop a rock, watching her. "Are you coming?" she snapped. She had no time for this. And not with Chay. Maybe she'd been delusional from the flu for the past day or so, but that hadn't changed things. He had Kimimela... And, dear God, did she remember something about a baby, too?

"We need to talk," he said, without budging.

"We're past talking, Chay. I know your little secret, and while I may have told you I loved you I can't have a relationship with someone who would turn his back on his own child."

"It's not my intention to turn my back."

"Not your intention?" Joanna stormed back over to confront him face-to-face. "That's all you've been doing for years, turning your back. She adores you, Chay. And she's been miserable since you left. I don't know how you could be so...so two-faced, being so wonderful with me and being such a good doctor, then abandoning your daughter like you did, especially now when she needs you so much."

"I don't have a daughter," he said, his voice so patient Joanna suddenly wondered if he didn't know.

"Donna Rousseau? Kimi?"

He shook his head. "I never even met Donna until the night she died."

"But I thought... Your father told me..."

"What, Joanna? What did my father tell you?"

"He asked me if you would assume responsibility for our child, so naturally I thought... I mean, you and Kimi seem to have such a bond, and she's the right age. What else was I supposed to think, Chay? Do you have a child?''

He nodded, but didn't speak.

''A baby.'' The baby she thought she'd dreamed about.

He nodded again. ''And I am its father, Joanna. All the way. From the beginning to the end.''

''You never told me. Is that why you stay in Chicago, why you won't come home?''

''But I have come home. To marry the mother of my baby, if she'll have me, and to be its father.''

Joanna sat down in the dirt in front of Chay. ''OK, I'm a little lost here.'' Unconsciously, she rubbed her hand over her belly. ''I know I've just been a fling to you, someone waiting in the wings while you've been having a real relationship—''

''Not a fling. It's been a real relationship, Joanna, and only with you. When I told you I loved you I meant it, and I'd made my decision before I knew that you were…''

''What, Chay? Before you knew that I was what?''

''Pregnant.''

It took several seconds for it to sink in before she could respond. ''What do you mean, I'm pregnant? I haven't had a pregnancy test.''

''Maybe not, but you are.'' He smiled. ''I think it happened that night here on the butte, which is why I had to bring you back here. You were filled with a deep brooding… And, yeah, I know that's not exactly a medical diagnosis. But that's what it was, Joanna, I swear to you. A deep brooding about something, and it was taking away your energy. Shaman stuff, I suppose. And now I understand why. You thought that Kimimela was my daughter, and that I'd abandoned her—twice, actually. And that you'd fallen in love with someone who could do something like that.'

''But your father said—''

"He was talking about our child, Joanna. The baby you're carrying inside you now."

"He couldn't know. Your father couldn't have known." This just didn't make sense. Leonard knew, and Chay knew. And there had been no test to confirm her pregnancy. But somehow, deep down, she believed Chay, and Leonard, because she remembered that moment, waking up on the floor, hearing Chay and Macawi talking about his baby and feeling for an instant it was her baby, too. Then she'd felt so sad and empty when she'd believed they'd been talking about someone else...someone else who was carrying Chay's child. "Could he?"

Chay slipped off the rock and sat cross-legged on the ground in front of Joanna, then laid his hand on her belly. And smiled. "He knew."

She glanced at the stone bowl—the same one Leonard had used in Michael Red Elk's extraction. "You went against everything you believe in," she said, laying her hand over his. "You performed a shaman rite for me."

"Everything I believe in is you, Joanna. You and our family. I knew what was bothering you was spiritual more than medical, more than what *our* kind of medicine could cure." He chuckled. "And as much as I hate to admit it, this was the only thing I could think of."

"Apparently it worked, because I'm feeling great." Better than great. "But what about Chicago, Chay? Your life there? Your new job?"

"Believe me, I've had second and third and fourth thoughts about this, but what I'm telling you is the truth. I wanted that life, that job. I worked hard to get it, but none of it matters now. And I'm not saying that because you're pregnant and I'm trying to do the right thing by you. That's not it at all. Before my dad told me, I'd already realized that everything I wanted was here. You, this life. And it scares the hell out of me, but this is all there is, Joanna, and

I wanted to tell you, but you've been in a pretty bad mood lately and it never seemed like the right time."

"Can you survive here, Chay? I know you have some awfully bad feelings. And this whole situation with your father…"

"This situation with my father will work out. But you're going to have to be patient with me because I can be—"

"Stubborn," she supplied. "Just like your father." And like her child? She rubbed her hand over her belly again. "So, where do we begin?"

"Well, I've been doing some thinking, and the first thing we need to do, after the White Eagles expand the clinic, is buy our own helicopter. The RV is nice when there's not an emergency, but we need something faster. And with a baby on the way we can't spend so much time on the road. So I've been investigating a place in Billings where I can take flying lessons, and I think that I'll give them a call in the next day or so. After I've finalized the plans for the clinic's expansion. Oh, and I was thinking about a wedding gift, assuming you are going to marry me. Are you?"

Joanna nodded, too overwhelmed to speak. This was so much more than she'd ever expected, and everything she wanted. Chay, their baby…

"Good. I was thinking our kid would like to have a big sister. And even though she's not my daughter, I would like to change that and welcome Little Butterfly into our family. If that's OK with you."

"That's OK," she said, squeezing his hand. At long last Joanna had her family. A perfect family. "Very OK."

June

"He's all red," Kimimela squealed, holding on to Chay' hand. "Can't you fix that, Daddy?"

"He's supposed to be that way. I'll bet you looked jus

like Leo when you were born.'' Chayton Leonard Ducheneaux, to be called Leo.

Kimi scrunched up her nose and darted into the hall to wait with her grandparents, Wenona and Leonard. And Macawi, who was busy knitting her fiftieth pair of blue bootees.

''How's Billy Begay?'' Joanna asked, pulling back her hospital gown and preparing herself to feed Leo.

''His last A1C was seven. I'd say he's keeping it under control pretty well.''

''And the Whirlwinds?''

''Better, but not great. My dad is going up next week to have a talk with them, give them some nutritional instruction on their diet.'' He smiled. ''And he's planning on doing the same at the ranch. Maybe starting a diabetic support group.'' These days the talking was still sparse between them, but Chay and Leonard did talk, most often about the Hawk Reservation diabetes awareness program Leonard had taken on as his cause.

''A true mixing of medical traditions.'' Joanna placed Leo to her breast, then looked up at Chay. ''It's going to work,'' she said, beaming. ''You, me, our children, our medical practice. It's all going to work.''

Chay bent down and placed a kiss on Leo's cheek, then one on Joanna's. Some things never changed. The old road leading from nowhere, going to nowhere was still dusty and desolate. The weather-beaten sign reading WELCOME TO HAWK RESERVATION, POPULATION 3000 hadn't seen a coat of paint on its gray, rotting boards since the first time he'd left here almost nineteen years ago. The rusty old hull of a 1972 Ford pickup truck that had been sitting off to the side of the road for the past nine years was still there.

No, some things never changed, but some things did. And they changed in amazing ways, ways he'd never expected, ways he'd never thought he'd be so lucky to know. Kimimela, Leo, Joanna…his family. They were everything he'd ever wanted, and that was one of those things on Hawk Reservation, his only home, that would never, ever change.

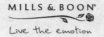

MILLS & BOON®
0605/03b

Live the emotion

_Medical romance™

A SPECIAL KIND OF CARING by *Jennifer Taylor*

Dr Francesca Goodwin wants to escape – from
London, from the pain of her last relationship, from
people. Working as a GP in isolated Teesdale sounds
perfect – until she meets her new partner, Dr Alex
Shepherd. He's good-looking, caring – and attracted
to her!

THE FLIGHT DOCTOR'S LIFELINE by *Laura Iding*

(Air Rescue)

Helicopter pilot Reese Jarvis is drawn to Dr Samantha
Kearn from the moment he sees her in action with the
Lifeline Medical Air Transport team. When he learns
she is having trouble with her ex-husband, he
immediately wants to protect her. He becomes her
lifeline, her support – but ever since his fiancée died he
has been reluctant to put his feelings on the line…

THE BUSH DOCTOR'S RESCUE by *Leah Martyn*

Nurse Ally Inglis doesn't know why Dr Marc Ballantyne
has come to the Outback town of Hillcrest, she's just
grateful to have a full-time doctor at last. Marc charms
and surprises everyone – not least of all Ally. He stirs
up feelings she thought she'd never have again. But she
can't help wondering, does this modern-day knight *really*
mean to rescue her heart…?

On sale 1st July 2005

*Available at most branches of WHSmith, Tesco, ASDA, Martins,
Borders, Eason, Sainsbury's and all good paperback bookshops.*

Visit www.millsandboon.co.uk

MILLS & BOON

Volume 12
on sale from
4th June
2005

Lynne
Graham
International Playboys

Tempestuous

Reunion

On sale 1st July 2005

Available at most branches of WHSmith, Tesco, ASDA, Martins, Borders, Eason, Sainsbury's and all good paperback bookshops.

FREE!

4 Books
and a surprise gift!

We would like to take this opportunity to thank you for reading this Mills & Boon® book by offering you the chance to take FOUR more specially selected titles from the Medical Romance™ series absolutely FREE! We're also making this offer to introduce you to the benefits of the Reader Service™—

- ★ **FREE home delivery**
- ★ **FREE gifts and competitions**
- ★ **FREE monthly Newsletter**
- ★ **Exclusive Reader Service offers**
- ★ **Books available before they're in the shops**

Accepting these FREE books and gift places you under no obligation to buy, you may cancel at any time, even after receiving your free shipment. Simply complete your details below and return the entire page to the address below. You don't even need a stamp!

YES! Please send me 4 free Medical Romance books and a surprise gift. I understand that unless you hear from me, I will receive 6 superb new titles every month for just £2.75 each, postage and packing free. I am under no obligation to purchase any books and may cancel my subscription at any time. The free books and gift will be mine to keep in any case.

M5ZEF

Ms/Mrs/Miss/Mr ....Initials.................................
BLOCK CAPITALS PLEASE
Surname ....
Address...

....Postcode ....

Send this whole page to:
UK: FREEPOST CN81, Croydon, CR9 3WZ